Something strikes me when I leaf through the pages o[...] old, yellowed and tattered *Tinkle* comics. It was called [...] Readers' Mail then and is called *Tinkle* Energy Meter n[...] Readers have changed over the years as they've grown [...] older and passed on their comics to younger siblings, or [...] in many cases to their children and sometimes to their grandchildren. There are some who have travelled with *Tinkle* on its journey. Yet the energy with which readers wrote and still write to *Tinkle* remains the same.

There is that same tone of joy when a joke tickles or that sense of accomplishment when an info-feature helps in school projects. There is that scold for a story that didn't satisfy or when a loved story or feature is found missing.

And more than any of these are the suggestions that pour in. In the older *Tinkle*s, there are suggestions to Uncle Pai about featuring rare creatures on the pages of animal features. Children have also urged *Tinkle* to publish new discoveries and inventions. One child suggested the inclusion of a holiday special book with more pages, stories, activities and puzzles.

You know what is remarkable? Uncle Pai and his team read every letter that was sent, replied to them and took note of the suggestions. This is why today we do have a series of books specially created for the holidays called... the *Holiday Special*!

Today, if *Tinkle* has more female characters, more superheroes or a *Tinkle Awards* which gets readers to vote for the best content of the year, it's because all these ideas had their germ in a mail or letter written by a young reader. Our readers tell us when they think we have not done enough with a directness only seen in the young. They also give us their love with the abandon of innocence.

Yes, our young readers are smarter now, more aware for they are the children of the digital age. But then, the children of the 1980s would have hardly been content with street plays when they had the wonder of TV to explore.

The 1980s will remain golden in the memories of all those of us who waited eagerly to watch *Chaayageet* and *Chitrahaar* on Doordarshan or greedily slurped on ice pops we blithely called 'pepsi'. And one of these golden memories is curling up with *Tinkle* comics. Here's to reliving those wonderfully innocent days.

Happy reading,

Rajani Thindiath
Editor-in-Chief, *Tinkle*

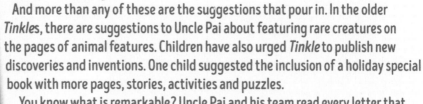

EDITOR-IN-CHIEF :	RAJANI THINDIATH
GROUP ART DIRECTOR :	SAVIO MASCARENHAS
EDITORIAL TEAM :	SEAN D'MELLO, APARNA SUNDARESAN, RITU MAHIMKAR, MAHZBEEN KAYANI, JUBEL D'CRUZ, POOJA WAGHELA
DESIGN TEAM :	TEJAS KOLHE, KETAN TONDWALKAR, RUBINA KADER
COVER DESIGN :	AKSHAY KHADILKAR
HEAD OF CREATIVE SERVICES :	KURIAKOSE SAJU VAISIAN

© Amar Chitra Katha Pvt. Ltd., November 2018, Reprinted August 2020
ISBN 978-93-87304-81-9
Published by Amar Chitra Katha Pvt. Ltd., 7th Floor, AFL House, Lok Bharati Complex,
Marol Maroshi Road, Andheri (East), Mumbai – 400059, India
Tel: +91 22 4918 888 1/2
www.tinkle.in | www.amarchitrakatha.com
Printed in India

Get in touch with us:

✉ tinklemail@ack-media.com ⊕ www.tinkleonline.com
🐦 @TinkleMagazine ⊕ www.amarchitrakatha.com
f Tinkle Comics Studio ⊕ www.tinkle.in
📷 @tinklecomicsstudio 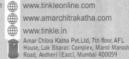 Amar Chitra Katha Pvt.Ltd, 7th floor, AFL House, Lok Bharati Complex, Marol Maroshi Road, Andheri (East), Mumbai 400059

INDEX

INDEX

THE WINNER

— A folktale from Haryana

Script:
Vibha Ghai
Illustrations:
Chandrakant Rane

ONCE THREE FRIENDS WERE PASSING THROUGH A JUNGLE.

IT'S GETTING DARK, LET'S REST HERE AND...

...HAVE SOME FOOD.

THEY STOPPED AND COOKED SOME KHEER.

SO AM I!

I WISH THE KHEER WOULD COOL FASTER. I'M DYING OF HUNGER.

I COULD FINISH THAT WHOLE POT OF KHEER.

SO COULD I!

I'LL TELL YOU WHAT. LET'S HAVE A SHORT NAP WHILE IT COOLS. THE ONE WHO HAS THE BEST DREAM SHALL HAVE ALL THE KHEER.

THAT'S A GOOD IDEA!

LET'S LIE DOWN RIGHT AWAY AND START DREAMING!

AND THAT'S WHAT THEY DID.

A LITTLE BEFORE DAWN ONE OF THEM WOKE UP.

AAH! THAT WAS A GOOD NAP! HAVE I FORGOTTEN SOMETHING...?

AH! THE DREAM! THE KHEER!

3

HEY! WHY ARE YOU SHOUTING?

THE KHEER, MY FRIEND...

AH, YES, THE DREAM! I HAD A....

WAIT! LET'S WAKE UP OUR FRIEND.

GET UP, FRIEND! WE'RE VERY HUNGRY.

GOOD! NOW YOU CAN TELL US YOUR DREAM.

I HAD A LOVELY DREAM.

"I FLOATED UP INTO THE CLOUDS AND GOT A GLIMPSE OF HEAVEN!"

I WAS ABOUT TO ENTER THE GATES OF HEAVEN WHEN I WOKE UP.

THEN I'VE DONE BETTER THAN YOU!

IN MY DREAM I WAS RIGHT INSIDE HEAVEN SEATED NEXT TO INDRA...

"...WATCHING THE HEAVENLY BEAUTIES DANCE."

YOU HAVE DONE BETTER THAN ME! YOU DESERVE THE KHEER.

YOU FORGET OUR FRIEND HERE! MAYBE HE HAD AN EVEN BETTER DREAM.

NO, MY FRIENDS. I HAD A TERRIBLE DREAM!

AN ANGRY LORD HANUMAN ORDERED ME TO EAT ALL THE KHEER, OR ELSE...

OR ELSE?

HE WOULD KILL ME, HE SAID.

THEN?

THEN WHAT? I HAD TO EAT ALL THE KHEER.

WHAT!

HOW DARE YOU!

YOU COULD HAVE WOKEN US UP, YOU CHEAT!

HOW COULD I?

BOTH OF YOU WERE IN HEAVEN AT THAT TIME.

5

Kalia
THE CROW

Script:
LUIS

Illustrations:
PRADEEP SATHE

WHAT! BIRDS HOPPING IN AND OUT OF DOOB-DOOB'S MOUTH!

WHAT WERE THEY DOING? WHY DID YOU LET THEM GO?

THEY ARE MY FRIENDS.

THEY WERE CLEANING MY TEETH... SEE...

WHY DIDN'T YOU CATCH AND EAT THEM WHEN THEY HAD FINISHED?

WHAT!

YOU THINK I WOULD EAT MY OWN FRIENDS?

WHY NOT?

I...I MEAN ONE SHOULD NOT EAT VERY GOOD FRIENDS LIKE ME, BUT BIRDS...

6

PUNYAKOTI

- A folktale from Karnataka,

Script:
Subba Rao
Illustrations:
K. Chandranath

HULIA THE TIGER WAS WEAK WITH HUNGER.

HE HAD NOT EATEN ANYTHING FOR DAYS.

IF I DON'T FIND SOME FOOD TODAY, I'LL DIE OF HUNGER.

JUST THEN—

TIN-TIN

WHAT'S THAT?

THE CATTLE RETURNING HOME AFTER GRAZING!

WHAT'S WRONG WITH ME? I COULDN'T CATCH A SILLY COW!

WHO DO I SEE COMING THIS WAY?

9

IT WAS A COW CALLED PUNYAKOTI.

I'D BETTER WALK FASTER. MY CHILD MUST BE WAITING FOR ME.

EH!

YES, I'VE BEEN WAITING FOR YOU.

HULIA, PLEASE LISTEN...

NO! I WON'T!

I AM GOING TO KILL YOU AND EAT YOU UP.

KILL ME! EAT ME! BUT NOT IMMEDIATELY.

MY CHILD IS WAITING FOR ME. I'LL GO HOME, FEED HIM AND COME BACK TO YOU.

WHAT!

HOHOHO!

DO YOU TAKE ME FOR A FOOL?

AS IF YOU'LL COME BACK, IF I LET YOU GO!

Punyakoti ran to her home at the foot of the hill.

Punyakoti told him everything about her promise to Hulia.

I MUST GO. I PROMISED HIM THAT I WOULD RETURN.

TRUTH IS MY MOTHER. TRUTH IS MY FATHER. TRUTH IS MY GOD. TRUTH IS EVERYTHING TO ME.

BUT MOTHER, WHO WILL FEED ME WHEN I'M HUNGRY? WHO WILL TAKE CARE OF ME?

MY SISTERS, TREAT THIS ORPHAN AS YOUR CHILD.

PLEASE DON'T GORE HIM WITH YOUR HORNS IF HE COMES IN YOUR WAY AND PLEASE DON'T KICK HIM IF HE IS AT YOUR BACK.

O PUNYAKOTI!

PUNYAKOTI, WE WILL ALL COME WITH YOU TO HULIA.

PLEASE DON'T. I WANT YOU TO TAKE CARE OF MY CHILD.

AS PUNYAKOTI LEFT—

MOTHER DON'T GO! PLEASE DON'T GO. MOTHER...

MEANWHILE HULIA WAS GETTING IMPATIENT.

I SHOULDN'T HAVE LET HER GO.

SHE'LL NEVER COME...NO, THERE SHE IS!

SHE HAS KEPT HER PROMISE...EVEN THOUGH DEATH AWAITS HER HERE. WHAT A NOBLE CREATURE!

HULIA, MY BROTHER, COME! HERE I AM. EAT ME.

EAT YOU?

NEVER, MY NOBLE SISTER. NEVER.

GO BACK TO YOUR CHILD.

HULIA!

HULIA TURNED BACK AND LEFT.

AND PUNYAKOTI REJOINED HER CHILD.

A BEAR ON A TREE

- A Nasruddin Hodja tale

Script: Devenshu Mohapatra
Illustrations: Ram Waeerkar

ONE DAY THE HODJA WAS WALKING THROUGH A FOREST WHEN HE SAW A BEAR COMING TOWARDS HIM.

HE HASTILY CLIMBED UP THE NEAREST TREE...

...AND WAITED FOR THE BEAR TO PASS BY.

UNFORTUNATELY, THE BEAR CHOSE THAT VERY TREE...

...TO SLEEP UNDER.

THE POOR HODJA SPENT THE WHOLE AFTERNOON ON THE TOP OF THE TREE. THEN TOWARDS EVENING—

HE'S GETTING UP AT LAST! OH, WHAT A RELIEF!

EH!

OH, MY GOD! HE'S CLIMBING UP!

THE BEAR WAS HUNGRY AND HAD CLIMBED UP TO EAT FRUITS.

HE'S COMING AFTER ME. I'D BETTER CLIMB TO THE HIGHEST BRANCH!

CHOMP CHOMP

BUT AFTER SOME TIME, THE BEAR TOO REACHED THAT SAME BRANCH.

NOW IT'S OVER FOR ME!

THIS IS MY LAST DAY ON EARTH.

HE IS OFFERING ME FRUITS!

I NEVER EAT FRUITS. THANK YOU.

?!

THE BEAR HAD NOT SEEN THE HODJA TILL THEN. HE WAS SO STARTLED BY THE SUDDEN APPEARANCE OF A HUMAN...

...THAT HE LOST HIS BALANCE.

...AND FELL.

CRASH

THEN PICKING HIMSELF UP, HE RAN AWAY AS FAST AS HE COULD.

HE'S GONE! THANK GOD!

BUT I CAN'T IMAGINE WHY HE WAS SO FRIGHTENED OF ME!

My young friends,
The very first story that was sent to me for our readers' choice section was about a Dove and an Ant. It was sent in by Master Sailesh of Bombay. An ant falls into a stream and is carried away from the bank. He struggles hard to get back to the bank. A kind-hearted dove, perched on a tree, sees him and throws a leaf down to him. The ant manages to climb onto the leaf and reaches the shore alive.
Had the dove known the Japanese art of Origami, he could have made the ant's journey not only safe but also comfortable! I'm sure that's what will strike you, when you've made the first model in our new series on Origami.
We will be holding a special workshop on Origami for our readers in Bombay. It will be held on a Sunday. Smt. Indu Tilak and Smt. Gita Kantawala will make some models and then help you to make them yourselves.
Those of you who would like to attend the workshop may write to me for more details.*

Affectionately yours,

Uncle Pai

* Refer to the footnote under the Editor's Note

ORIGAMI

JAPANESE PAPERCRAFT

Would you believe that all these beautiful models have been made by just folding a piece of paper? That you could make them too? Turn to your TTT page and you will find a new treat awaiting you.

Trace these signs and symbols onto a piece of paper. Paste the paper on a card and keep it handy before you start working on the models that TTT will bring you from time to time.

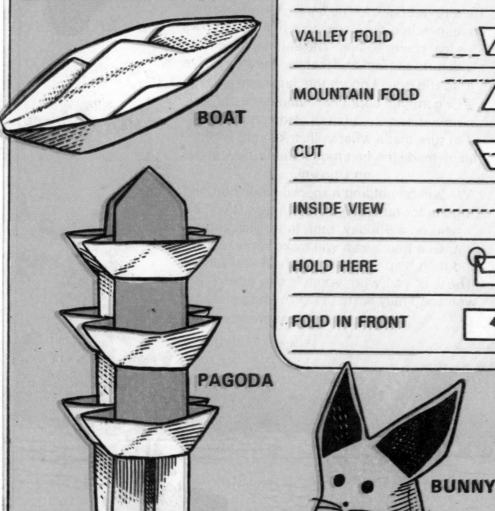

BOAT

PAGODA

BUNNY

VALLEY FOLD	
MOUNTAIN FOLD	
CUT	
INSIDE VIEW	
HOLD HERE	
FOLD IN FRONT	

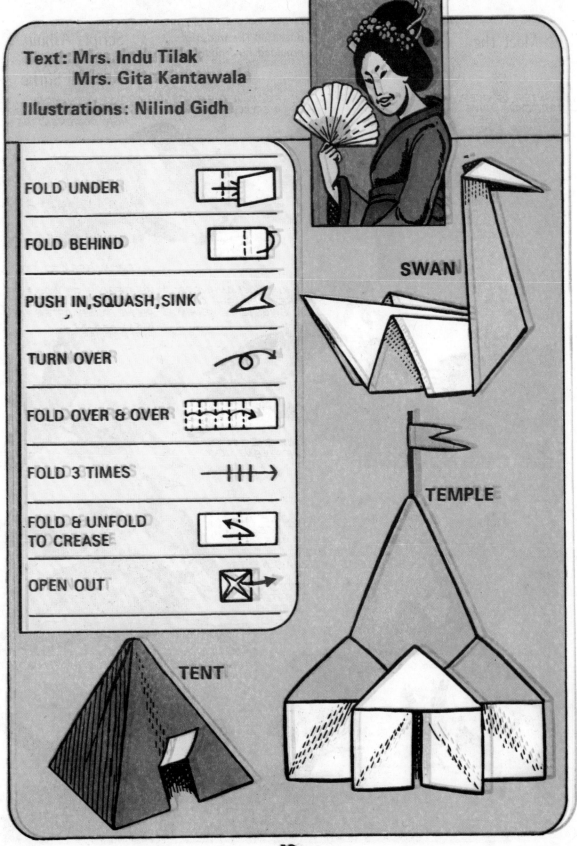

Text: Mrs. Indu Tilak
      Mrs. Gita Kantawala

Illustrations: Nilind Gidh

FOLD UNDER

FOLD BEHIND

PUSH IN, SQUASH, SINK

TURN OVER

FOLD OVER & OVER

FOLD 3 TIMES

FOLD & UNFOLD TO CREASE

OPEN OUT

SWAN

TEMPLE

TENT

Meet the *Koel*

Based on the material provided by Nandini Deshmukh

Script: Ashvin
Illustrations: Pradeep Sathe

WINTER IS OVER. THE DAYS HAVE BEGUN TO GET WARMER. EARLY ONE MORNING YOU HEAR A BIRD CALL KU-OO! KU-OO! SIX OR SEVEN TIMES, HIS VOICE GETTING SHRILLER WITH EACH CALL. IT'S THE KOEL.

FROM A DISTANCE HE LOOKS VERY MUCH LIKE A CROW. BUT WHEN HE COMES CLOSER YOU SEE HOW DIFFERENT HE IS...

...FROM BEAK TO FOOT.

KU-OO! KU-OO! I'M LOOKING FOR A MATE, HE COOS.

KIK-KIK-KIK! ANSWERS A SHE KOEL. SHE CAN'T COO SWEETLY LIKE HIM.

HE BEGINS TO WOO HER. KU-OO! KU-OO! HE COOS, AS HE FLIES AFTER HER. KIK-KIK-KIK! SHE REPLIES.

AND SHE LOOKS DIFFERENT TOO.

HE HAS WON HER! SEE HOW LOVING HE IS! WHY, HE EVEN PUTS FOOD INTO HER MOUTH.

SHE'S SOON GOING TO NEED A NEST. KOELS DON'T BUILD THEIR OWN NESTS. THEY LAY THEIR EGGS IN CROWS' NESTS.

THE MALE SPOTS ONE WITH A BATCH OF NEW-LAID EGGS. HE CLEVERLY LETS THE CROWS SEE HIM.

WHILE THEY'RE BUSY CHASING HIM AWAY...

...HIS MATE FLIES INTO THE UNGUARDED NEST AND LAYS AN EGG.

THEN SHE FLIES AWAY AND FORGETS ALL ABOUT IT.

YOU CAN SEE THE EGG HERE. IT LOOKS SO MUCH LIKE THE EGGS OF THE CROW...

...THAT WHEN MOTHER CROW COMES BACK SHE TAKES IT TO BE ONE OF HER OWN, AND HATCHES IT ALONG WITH THEM.

ON THE THIRTEENTH DAY, THE BABY KOEL COMES OUT. MOTHER KOEL HAS TIMED IT WELL!

MOTHER CROW'S EGGS HATCH ONLY THREE OR FOUR DAYS LATER. BY THEN BABY KOEL IS BIGGER AND STRONGER THAN THE BABY CROWS. SHE CAN RAISE HER NECK OFTENER AND HIGHER TO GRAB THE FOOD HER FOSTER-PARENTS BRING.

IN FACT SHE GRABS MOST OF THE FOOD THEY BRING!

BECAUSE OF THIS SOME OF THE CROW'S OWN BABIES DIE OF STARVATION.

WHEN THE KOEL HAS LEARNED TO FLY, SHE GOES OFF ON HER OWN.

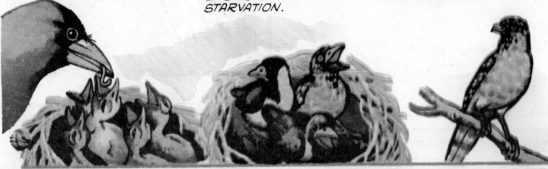

THE KOEL IS USEFUL TO FARMERS BECAUSE IT EATS CATERPILLARS WHICH DAMAGE CROPS.

THIS BIRD TOO, NEVER BUILDS ITS OWN NEST. WHEN IT ADDS AN EGG TO ANOTHER BIRD'S NEST, IT REMOVES ONE OR TWO OF THAT BIRD'S EGGS. EVEN THE NEW-HATCHED CUCKOO SQUIRMS ITSELF UNDER THE OTHER EGGS IN THE NEST AND PUSHES THEM OVER THE RIM ONE BY ONE.

THE COMMON CUCKOO
(FOUND IN EURASIA, AFRICA)

TINKLE TRICKS & TREATS TTT-18

B | Where should the flower go in the last frame?

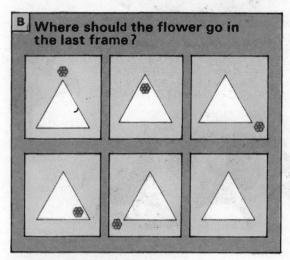

A | Identify the animals

1

2

3

4

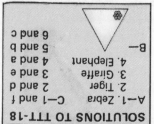

SOLUTIONS TO TTT-18

A—1. Zebra   C—1 and f
2. Tiger   2 and d
3. Giraffe   3 and e
4. Elephant   4 and a
B—   5 and b
6 and c

C | Match the ornament and the part of the body on which it is worn.

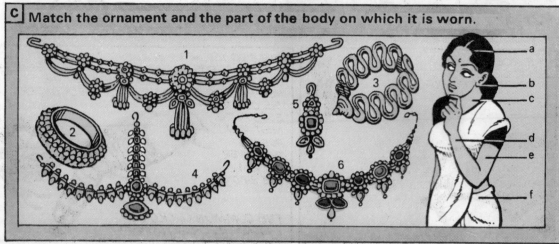

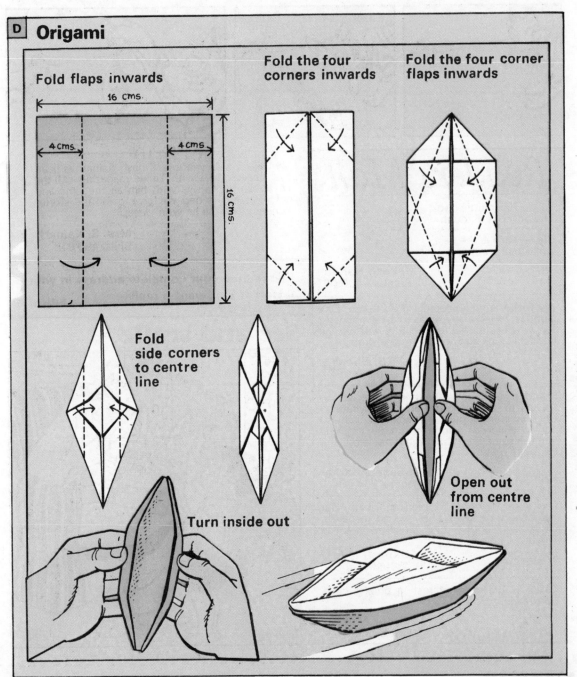

Fold flaps inwards

16 cms.

4 cms.   4 cms.

16 cms.

Fold the four corners inwards

Fold the four corner flaps inwards

Fold side corners to centre line

Open out from centre line

Turn inside out

* Refer to the footnote under the Editor's Note

RULES*

1. Mail your entries (entry form given overleaf) to :
   Tinkle (Competition Section). Post Box No. 1382, Bombay 400001.

2. With your entry you could send a self-addressed stamped (35 paise) envelope and collect an animal sticker. You will also receive a yellow label if yours is an all-correct entry.

3. When you collect **3** such labels you could exchange them for a colourful animal mask.

Mooshik

Readers' Mail

Tinkle Tinkle little book,
The only one through which I look,

Clever Kalia is the best,
Dull Doob Doob is a pest.

Rakesh Handa
Bombay-400 061

My friend is still sleeping at 8.00 a.m. One Sunday, I tried many times to awake him. At last when I shouted that TINKLE was out, he suddenly woke up and ran to the shop.

T.S. Shankar
Hyderabad-27

I find that Tinkle is the only comic which listens to children. It publishes whatever children want. It publishes whatever is helpful to children. I hope next time you will publish something about oil. What is oil, and its uses?

Debashis Sarkar
Ranchi-834 004

I am short of words for praising Tinkle. Our neighbours just won't let me sit in peace, unless and until I give them my beloved Tinkle.

Ganesh Iyer
Valsad-396 020

Tinkle is the most interesting book I have ever read.

Victor Moktan
East Sikkim

My little son 4½ year old Brijesh Kamath is head over heels in love with Tinkle magazine...All the 14 books he carries with him all the time and before going to bed we have to tell the stories to him otherwise he won't sleep.

Mrs. S. Kamath
Bhilai 490 010

Please give your complete address in your letters if you want a reply.

-Editor

See and smile

-CUT HERE-----

ENTRY FORM*

NAME_____

ADDRESS_____

_____

_____

PIN ☐☐☐☐☐☐

MY SOLUTIONS:

A1_____

2_____

3_____

4_____

B

C 1 and_____

2 and_____

3 and_____

4 and_____

5 and_____

6 and_____

TTT-18

24

THE TORTOISE BAND

From our reader Laxmikant Kolwalkar, Bombay
Illustrations: V.B. Halbe

ONE DAY A LEOPARD CALLED A MEETING OF ALL THE ANIMALS OF THE JUNGLE.

WE NEED A KING.

AND WHO WOULD MAKE A BETTER KING THAN ME?

I AM HANDSOME, BRAVE AND CLEVER.

NO ONE CAN DO ANYTHING BETTER OR FASTER THAN I CAN. RIGHT?

WRONG. THERE ARE SOME THINGS THAT I CAN DO FASTER AND BETTER THAN YOU.

OH! CAN YOU?

AND WHAT MAY THEY BE?

BUILDING A HOUSE, FOR EXAMPLE. I COULD DO THAT MUCH FASTER THAN YOU.

WHEN DO WE BEGIN THE CONTEST?

RIGHT AWAY, YOU MAY TAKE THE HELP OF YOUR FRIENDS, AND I'LL TAKE THE HELP OF MINE.

AGREED.

THE LEOPARD JOINED HIS PACK AND GAVE ORDERS.

I WANT YOU TO RUN TO THE RIVERSIDE. YOU BRING THE MUD, YOU THE STONES AND YOU...

THE TORTOISE TOO GOT BUSY TELLING HIS FRIENDS WHAT TO DO.

DON'T TAKE WATER FROM THE RIVER USED BY THE LEOPARDS. GO TO THE OTHER RIVER.

WE'LL DO ANYTHING TO BUILD YOUR HOUSE FAST.

WE WANT YOU FOR OUR KING AND NOT THAT VAIN LEOPARD.

BUT WILL WE SUCCEED?

WE WILL IF YOU STOP TALKING AND START WORKING.

HERE WE GO.

THEN THE OLD TORTOISE TURNED TO HIS YOUNG ONES.

YOU, OF COURSE, KNOW WHAT YOU HAVE TO DO. GO. DO IT WELL.

THE LITTLE ONES EACH PICKED UP A LITTLE DRUM...

...AND MARCHED OFF TO THE RIVER WHERE THE LEOPARDS WERE AT WORK.

SOON— MUSIC! DRUM-BEATS!

HEY! WHY ARE WE DANCING?

I DON'T KNOW. BUT I CAN'T STOP DANCING.

MEANWHILE THE LEOPARD WAS GETTING IMPATIENT.

GO AND SEE WHY THOSE RASCALS ARE TAKING SO LONG.

TELL THEM TO COME BACK QUICKLY WITH THE MUD AND STONES.

HOURS PASSED. THE CUBS DID NOT COME BACK.

IT'S ALMOST EVENING. AND WE HAVEN'T EVEN BEGUN WORK ON THE HOUSE.

THE LEOPARD HIMSELF WENT TO THE RIVERSIDE.

AND HE TOO BEGAN TO DANCE.

MY LEGS ARE ACHING.

I HAVE A SORE FOOT.

FASTER AND FASTER WENT THE MUSIC AND FASTER DANCED THE LEOPARDS.

PLEASE STOP THE MUSIC!

HAVE MERCY! PLEASE STOP IT.

MY HOUSE IS READY!

WHAT?

THE TORTOISE HAD WON! AS FOR THE LEOPARD, HE JUST SLUNK AWAY.

THANK YOU, O KING, FOR GETTING RID OF THAT PEST.

28

THE GENEROUS HOST

- A folktale from Tamil Nadu

Script: Luis M. Fernandes
Illustrations: Ram Waeerkar

ONCE UPON A TIME THERE WAS A POOR BUT GENEROUS MAN. ONE DAY—

THERE ARE SOME MEN OUTSIDE. THEY SAY YOU INVITED THEM TO LUNCH.

AH, YES!

I FORGOT TO TELL YOU ABOUT IT!

WHY ARE YOU ALWAYS INVITING PEOPLE TO LUNCH WHEN WE HAVE NOTHING TO OFFER THEM?

THERE IS NOT A GRAIN OF RICE IN THE HOUSE!

SSSSH! DON'T SHOUT! THEY MIGHT HEAR YOU!

DON'T WORRY ABOUT THE FOOD. I'LL GO OUT AND GET SOMETHING.

WELCOME, MY FRIENDS, WELCOME! PLEASE COME IN.

MAY WE VISIT THE TEMPLE FIRST?

29

CERTAINLY! FOOD WILL BE READY BY THE TIME YOU RETURN.

FOOD! HAH! HE'LL JUST WANDER AROUND AND COME BACK EMPTY-HANDED.

I'LL HAVE TO GET THOSE MEN TO LEAVE BEFORE HE RETURNS.

SOMETIME LATER WHEN THE GUESTS RETURNED —

COME IN, COME IN!

MY HUSBAND HAS JUST GONE OUT BUT HE'LL BE BACK SOON.

!

WHAT ARE YOU LOOKING AT?

OH! THAT! IT'S MY HUSBAND'S DEITY.

HE WORSHIPS A MORTAR AND PESTLE?!

30

HE DOES! AND I SHOULDN'T BE TELLING YOU THIS, BUT···

···WHEN HE COMES HOME, HE'LL PICK UP THAT PESTLE AND KNOCK ALL OF YOU ON THE HEADS WITH IT.

LET'S GET OUT OF HERE, BROTHERS.

THAT'S THE ONLY WAY OF PLEASING THIS DEITY.

THIS IS A MADHOUSE!

AS THE GUESTS RUSHED AWAY—

HEY!

WHAT'S THE MATTER? WHY ARE THEY GOING AWAY? AND THAT TOO IN SUCH A HURRY?

THEY ASKED ME FOR THIS PESTLE AND I DID NOT GIVE IT TO THEM.

WHAT!

YOU REFUSED TO GIVE OUR GUESTS AN ORDINARY PESTLE! SHAME ON YOU!

I'LL RUN AFTER THEM AND GIVE IT TO THEM.

COME BACK, FRIENDS, COME BACK.

LOOK!

HE'S COMING AFTER US WITH THE PESTLE!

HE'LL KNOCK US ON OUR HEADS!

RUN, BROTHERS, RUN!

THE MEN RAN AWAY AS FAST AS THEY COULD.

AND WHEN THEY REACHED THE TOWN THEY TOLD EVERYONE WHAT HAD HAPPENED.

...HE CHASED US WITH THE PESTLE FOR HALF A MILE.

I DID NOT KNOW HE WAS SUCH A CRUEL MAN.

NEITHER DID I.

AFTER THAT, MUCH TO HIS WIFE'S RELIEF NO ONE ACCEPTED THE POOR MAN'S INVITATIONS TO LUNCH ANY MORE.

NO. 17

Rs. 2.50

TINKLE

AMAR CHITRA KATHA

THE CHILDREN'S MONTHLY FROM THE HOUSE OF AMAR CHITRA KATHA

HOW THE MISER OUTSMARTED HIMSELF

THE MOON-GOD'S MESSENGER

GLASS

G.L. MIRCHANDANI & H.G. MIRCHANDANI

Mr. Ghanshyam Lilaram Mirchandani was the founder and chairman of India Book House Limited. His nephew, Mr. Hargobind Mirchandani was a director of the company. Mr. H.G. Mirchandani was responsible for the administration and finances of the company. At the time, India Book House was the largest distributor of periodicals, books and comics in India.

When Mr. Anant Pai thought of an Indian comic book, he first proposed the idea to Bennet Coleman and Co. Ltd. (the company that owns *The Times of India*). Following their lack of interest, he shared his idea with Mr. G.L. Mirchandani and Mr. H.G. Mirchandani. This was the birth of *Amar Chitra Katha*. The Mirchandanis were extremely supportive and encouraging of Mr. Pai's endeavour.

The Mirchandanis were also actively involved and interested in the different issues of *Amar Chitra Katha*. Every script, once approved by the Editorial Team, went around for everyone's opinion. Mr. Anant Pai, Mr. Subba Rao, Ms. Kamala Chandrakant, Mr. G.L. Mirchandani and Mr. H.G. Mirchandani signed their initials on the script as a mark of approval.

This system of a script making the rounds was followed until a year after *Tinkle* came into being. But both Mr. G.L. Mirchandani and Mr. H.G. Mirchandani remained enthusiastically involved in the activities of *Amar Chitra Katha* and *Tinkle*. They sponsored and participated in all promotional events and celebratory functions.

Mr. G.L. Mirchandani, as proprietor of India Book House, always had complete faith in Mr. Pai and gave him full freedom to develop *Amar Chitra Katha* and *Tinkle*. For the Mirchandanis as it was for Mr. Pai, *Amar Chitra Katha* was about their love for Indian culture and passion for stories.

Kalia
THE CROW

Script:
LUIS
Illustrations :
PRADEEP SATHE

OH, WHAT A BEAUTIFUL MORNING! I'LL TAKE A WALK IN THE JUNGLE!

GET OFF THE ROAD, YOU IDIOT!

?!

A TALKING BUSH!

I MUST BE THE FIRST ANIMAL ANY PLANT HAS SPOKEN TO.

I ALWAYS KNEW THERE WAS SOMETHING SPECIAL ABOUT ME.

PERHAPS IT IS MY NOBLE APPEARANCE WHICH MAKES ME SO POPULAR.

HELLO, DOOB—DOOB!

HELLO! HELLO! WHAT A BIG TREE YOU ARE!

ARE YOU TALKING TO THE TREE?

YOU! I THOUGHT...

KALIA, A BUSH SPOKE TO ME BACK THERE.

IT DID?

WHAT DID IT SAY?

IT SAID: GET OFF THE ROAD, YOU IDIOT!

I CAN GUESS WHO IS IN THAT BUSH.

WHAT A RUDE PLANT!

RUDE?

IT CALLED YOU AN IDIOT, DIDN'T IT?

GO BACK AND DEMAND AN APOLOGY.

I'LL DO THAT.

HOW DARE IT CALL ME AN IDIOT!

MEANWHILE—

AH, RABBITS!

IN A LITTLE WHILE THEY'LL BE CLOSE ENOUGH FOR ME TO POUNCE ON THEM.

OH, NO! THAT STUPID CROCODILE IS BACK!

I TOLD YOU TO GET OFF THE ROAD, DIDN'T I?

HOW DARE YOU TALK TO ME LIKE THAT

WHAM

THUD

WELL DONE!

WHO SAID THAT...?

OH, ANOTHER BUSH! HELLO, HELLO!

The chief and the glutton
—A Nepalese folktale

Illustrations: V.B. Halbe

Based on a story sent by
Suraj Ghising Lama
Jalpaiguri

THE CHIEF OF A VILLAGE BECAME FRIENDLY WITH ONE OF THE VILLAGERS. BUT AFTER SOME TIME HE FOUND THAT THE MAN WAS A GLUTTON.

HOW MUCH HE EATS! AND HE COMES EVERY DAY.

WE MUST STOP HIM FROM COMING SO OFTEN.

THE NEXT EVENING—

HE'LL BE HERE ANY MOMENT NOW I'M GOING OUT.

TELL HIM WE HAVE ALREADY EATEN AND SEND HIM AWAY AS POLITELY AS YOU CAN.

THE FRIEND CAME AS USUAL

HOW HUNGRY I AM!

I AM SORRY, I HAVE NOTHING TO OFFER YOU.

WE'VE ALREADY EATEN AND THE CHIEF HAS GONE OUT.

OH!

IF HE WERE HERE HE WOULD CERTAINLY HAVE KILLED A CHICKEN FOR YOU.

A CHICKEN!

I LOVE CHICKEN!

WHAT DOES IT MATTER IF THE CHIEF IS NOT AT HOME? I'LL CATCH A CHICKEN...

...AND YOU CAN COOK IT FOR ME.

NO, NO!

WHY NOT?

EH? WELL, I...ER...

...I CAN'T PUT A GUEST TO SUCH TROUBLE. MY HUSBAND WOULD GET TERRIBLY ANGRY.

NONSENSE! IT'S NO TROUBLE AT ALL!

GET EVERYTHING READY. I'LL CATCH THE CHICKEN.

SOON THE HELPLESS WOMAN FOUND HERSELF COOKING A FAT CHICKEN.

WHY DID I HAVE TO TALK OF CHICKENS! NOW WHAT WILL MY HUSBAND SAY?

SOMETIME LATER THE CHIEF CAME BACK.

DID HE...

··· COME ··· OH, HELLO ···

YOU'RE BACK!

I...ER...HAD TO GO OUT.

I KNOW, I KNOW! IT DOESN'T MATTER.

YOUR WIFE IS COOKING A DELICIOUS MEAL FOR ME. M-M-M-M!

I CAN'T WAIT TO EAT IT.

I'LL TELL HER TO HURRY UP.

WHAT HAPPENED?

EVERYTHING WENT WRONG.

HE INSISTED THAT I COOK A CHICKEN FOR HIM.

ALL RIGHT, NOW LISTEN...

...WHEN THE CHICKEN IS READY GIVE HIM ONLY TWO PIECES.

BUT SERVE THEM IN THE COPPER PLATE WHICH WE KEEP FOR GUESTS.

AND THE REST OF THE CHICKEN?

SERVE IT TO ME— IN AN ORDINARY CLAY POT.

WHEN THE CHICKEN WAS READY, THE WIFE DID AS HER HUSBAND HAD TOLD HER.

I ATE BEFORE GOING OUT BUT I'M HUNGRY AGAIN.

WHAT SORT OF MAN DO YOU TAKE ME FOR?

EH?

DO YOU THINK I WOULD LET YOU EAT OUT OF A CLAY POT? YOU ARE THE CHIEF!

COME, GIVE ME THAT POT AND TAKE THIS PLATE.

NO! NO!

I ALWAYS EAT OUT OF A CLAY POT AT HOME.

THAT'S RIGHT.

NOT IN MY PRESENCE, YOU WON'T!

WELL, ALL RIGHT. I'LL EAT OUT OF THE COPPER PLATE.

BUT I HOPE WE ARE NOT TROUBLED BY THE EVIL SPIRIT TODAY.

EVIL SPIRIT?

AN EVIL SPIRIT SOMETIMES COMES TO OUR HOUSE AND PUTS OUT THE LIGHT.

IS THAT SO?

I THINK I KNOW WHAT MY HUSBAND HAS IN MIND.

HEY!

WHOOSH!

IN THE DARKNESS, THE CHIEF TRIED TO EXCHANGE THE DISHES...

41

...BUT BEFORE HE COULD DO SO —

WHAM!

THE EVIL SPIRIT WAS TRYING TO STEAL MY CHICKEN, BUT I WAS TOO QUICK FOR HIM.

NOW IF YOU DON'T MIND I'LL FINISH MY DINNER ELSE-WHERE.

OOOOH!

GET UP... ARE YOU ALL RIGHT?

HE HAS GONE AWAY... WITH THE CHICKEN.

THE RASCAL... OUCH!

NEVER MIND! WE'LL FIND A WAY TO OUTWIT HIM TOMORROW.

How the horse was tamed

Story by Dr. S. Patel
Illustrations: Makara

ONE DAY LONG AGO, A STAG CAME TO THE PLACE WHERE A HORSE WAS GRAZING.

GO AWAY, THIS IS MY LAND!

THERE IS ENOUGH GRASS HERE FOR BOTH OF US.

GO AWAY, I SAID!

STAY WHERE YOU ARE!

ONE STEP FORWARD AND I'LL PIERCE YOU WITH MY ANTLERS.

THE STAG CAME EVERY DAY AND THE HORSE BECAME VERY ANGRY.

THEN ONE DAY HE WENT TO A HUNTER.

PLEASE COME AND SLAY A STAG FOR ME.

A STAG?

IT WILL RUN AWAY AS SOON AS IT SEES ME. AND STAGS RUN VERY FAST.

I CAN RUN FASTER. GET ON MY BACK, I'LL SHOW YOU.

NO! I'LL FALL OFF.

IF YOU TIE A ROPE ROUND MY MOUTH AND HOLD ON TO IT, YOU WON'T FALL OFF.

THE HUNTER DID AS THE HORSE SUGGESTED.

YOU ARE RIGHT. YOU CAN RUN VERY FAST. TAKE ME TO THE STAG.

WHEN THE STAG SAW THE HUNTER, IT TRIED TO RUN AWAY...

...BUT THE HUNTER CAUGHT UP WITH IT...

44

···AND —

WHOOSH!

HE IS DEAD!

NOW YOU MAY GET DOWN AND GO HOME.

YES. I'LL GO HOME.

BUT I AM TAKING YOU WITH ME, MY FRIEND. YOU HAVE SHOWN ME HOW USEFUL YOU CAN BE TO ME WHEN I GO HUNTING.

AND WHEN I AM NOT HUNTING YOU CAN HELP MY FATHER IN THE FIELDS.

NO! NO!

PLEASE LET ME GO!

THE HUNTER HOWEVER DID NOT LET HIM GO. AND EVER SINCE, THE HORSE HAS SERVED MAN.

KINDNESS TO ANIMALS

—A Nasruddin Hodja tale

Script: Luis M. Fernandes
Illustrations: Ram Waeerkar

ONE DAY HODJA BOUGHT A SACK OF VEGETABLES. HE LIFTED THE SACK ONTO HIS SHOULDER...

...MOUNTED HIS DONKEY...

...AND SET OFF FOR HOME. ON THE WAY HE MET A FRIEND.

WHY ARE YOU CARRYING THAT SACK ON YOUR BACK?

WHY DON'T YOU PLACE IT ON YOUR DONKEY?

THAT WOULD BE CRUEL.

I AM SO FAT AS IT IS...

...HOW CAN I LET THIS SMALL DONKEY CARRY BOTH ME AND THE SACK?

46

THREE MEN ON A TREE

READERS' CHOICE — Based on a story sent by Taran Sareen, Bombay. — Illustrations: Ram Waeerkar

HOLD ON, I'LL HELP YOU DOWN.

47

* Refer to the footnote under the Editor's Note

TINKLE TRICKS & TREATS
TTT-19

A This little girl wants exactly 17 of the flowers growing at the gaps to the centre of the lawn. You may pick flowers at any of the gaps but you must pick all the flowers at the gaps you choose to pass through. If you choose the gaps carefully you can take exactly 17 flowers to her.

Find the animals hiding in this picture.

Origami-Tumbling Joker — Mrs. Indu Tilak and Mrs. Gita Kantawala

Fold paper as shown.

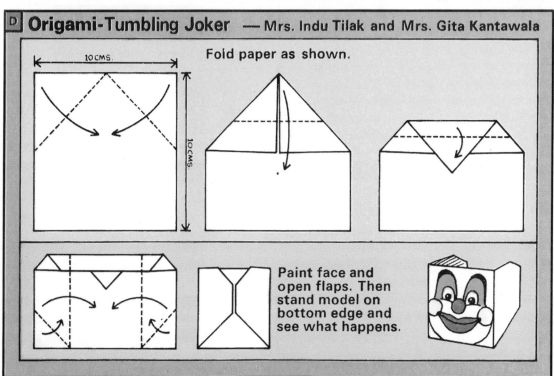

10 CMS.

10 CMS.

Paint face and open flaps. Then stand model on bottom edge and see what happens.

* Refer to the footnote under the Editor's Note

RULES*

1. Mail your entries (entry form given overleaf) to:
   Tinkle (Competition Section), Post Box No. 1382, Bombay 400001.

2. With your entry you could send a self-addressed stamped (**35** paise) envelope and collect an animal sticker. You will also receive a yellow label if yours is an all-correct entry.

3. When you collect **3** such labels you could exchange them for a colourful animal mask.

Mooshik

From an idea suggested by Babasaheb Taras, Ahmednagar.

Readers' Mail

Your Tinkle is becoming very popular month by month and I think that it would never stop. But why don't you make a separate book of Kalia the Crow?

Mandar S. Vaidya
Vishakhapatnam-8

I am very angry with my paper man because he gives me Tinkle late. Please from now onwards send Tinkle to Hyderabad very fast like lightning.

Ajay
Secunderabad 500 025.

When my parents say to study I quickly go and read Tinkle.

Akshay Mathur
New Delhi 110048

I went to a painting competition conducted by the Forest Department and in that I drew the Wild life from Tinkle (Kalia) and I got a second prize for it.

N. Vijay Varma
Hyderabad 50004

My friends tell me that in the Reader's Mail you (the editor) print letters yourself and put the names and the places. I think that it is not true.

Anal P. Bhagwati
Ahmedabad 380006

Do we have to send 6 coupons or 3 coupons to receive a colourful mask? In the TTT Gift coupon it is given that we have to send 6 coupons but in the issue No. 18 in the TTT rules it is given we have to send 3 coupons. Could you please tell me how many coupons to send?

A. Koushik Balaji
Madras

Those of you who send us 6 gift coupons will get two colourful masks and those who send us 3 gift coupons will get only one. —Editor

See and smile

Halbe

* Refer to the footnote under the Editor's Note

-CUT HERE- -

ENTRY FORM *

NAME _____

ADDRESS _____

_____

_____

_____ PIN ▢▢▢▢▢▢

MY SOLUTIONS:

A Gap 1 : _____ flowers

Gap 2 : _____ flowers

Gap 3 : _____ flowers

Gap 4 : _____ flowers

Gap 5 : _____ flowers

Total 17 flowers

B _____

TTT-19

C 1 _____

2 _____

3 _____

4 _____

5 _____

6 _____

51

MEET THE HIPPOPOTAMUS

Script: Ashvin
Illustrations: Pradeep Sathe

HUGE MR. HIPPO, WHO LIVES IN THE FORESTS OF AFRICA, HAS DECIDED TO COME OUT OF THE WATER HE LOVES TO LAZE IN. THE ONLY LAND ANIMAL BIGGER THAN HIM IS THE ELEPHANT.

AS HE WALKS ON, SHINY PATCHES APPEAR ON HIS SKIN. IT'S THE OIL HIS BODY SENDS OUT, TO KEEP HIS SKIN FROM BECOMING TOO DRY. THIS OIL ITSELF SLOWLY HARDENS AND PROTECTS HIS SKIN.

HE'S COME TO VISIT A FEMALE FRIEND!

FEMALE HIPPOS, AND THEIR YOUNG ONES LIVE TOGETHER. ADULT MALE HIPPOS LIVE AWAY FROM THEM AND FROM ONE ANOTHER.

AS HE APPROACHES, ONE OF THE FEMALES STANDS UP.

MR. HIPPO IMMEDIATELY LIES DOWN.

AH! SHE'S LYING DOWN!

HE GETS UP...

THAT'S THE RULE. HE MAY STAND UP AGAIN ONLY WHEN SHE LIES DOWN.

...AND MOVES FORWARD.

WHAT! ANOTHER FEMALE HAS STOOD UP!

BUT THIS TIME MR. HIPPO DOES NOT SIT DOWN. HE KEEPS WALKING.

ALL THE FEMALES, INCLUDING HIS FRIEND, AT ONCE GET UP AND DRIVE HIM AWAY. THEY WON'T TOLERATE BAD MANNERS.

CRAZY FEMALES! WELL, WHO CARES...

HUH, WHAT'S THIS? A MALE COMING TOWARDS HIM! DOES EVERYONE THINK THEY CAN TAKE ADVANTAGE OF HIS GOOD NATURE?

HE OPENS HIS MOUTH AND SHOWS HIS HUGE TUSKS. YOU MAY THINK HE IS YAWNING...

...BUT THE OTHER HIPPO KNOWS IT'S A WARNING. HE QUICKLY LOWERS HIS HEAD AND GOES OFF.

MR. HIPPO HAS HAD ENOUGH EXCITEMENT FOR ONE DAY. HE GOES BACK TO THE RIVER, LOWERS HIMSELF INTO IT...

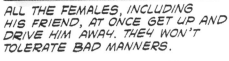

...CLOSES HIS NOSTRILS TIGHTLY AND ALLOWS HIMSELF TO SINK TO THE BOTTOM.

HERE HE IS WALKING ON THE BED OF THE RIVER, FEEDING ON THE PLANTS GROWING THERE. HE CAN STAY UNDER WATER FOR AS LONG AS TEN MINUTES.

THEN HE SLOWLY RISES TO THE SURFACE TO BREATHE.

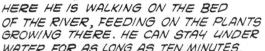

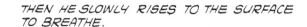

HE DOES NOT HAVE TO COME OUT OF THE WATER FOR THIS BECAUSE HIS NOSTRILS ARE AT THE TOP OF HIS SNOUT AND HIS EYES ARE HIGH UP ON HIS HEAD!

THE RIVER-BED CAN-NOT GIVE HIM ALL THE FOOD HE NEEDS. SO HE COMES OUT ON LAND AT NIGHT TO GIVE HIMSELF A GOOD FEED. HE IS A STRICT VEGETARIAN.

ONE DAY, A FEMALE WHO WANTS TO MATE, COMES TOWARDS HIM.

HE RECEIVES HER POLITELY.

AFTER MATING SHE GOES AWAY.

ABOUT EIGHT MONTHS LATER, SHE GOES OFF ALONE TO A SECLUDED SPOT AND GIVES BIRTH TO A CALF.

IT IS 90 CMS. LONG, 45 CMS. TALL, AND CAN WALK AND RUN FIVE MINUTES AFTER IT IS BORN.

IT CAN EVEN SWIM. BUT IT HAS TO SWIM ALONGSIDE ITS MOTHER'S SHOULDER.

IF IT FAILS TO OBEY THIS RULE, IT IS PUNISHED. THE MOTHER LASHES AT IT WITH HER HEAD.

BUT IF HER CALF IS TIRED OR IF ENEMIES LIKE CROCODILES ARE AROUND, SHE GIVES HER BABY A RIDE ON HER BACK.

HERE SHE IS, BACK WITH THE OTHER FEMALES.

FEMALE HIPPOS LOOK AFTER THE CALF OF ANY MOTHER WHO WANTS TO GO OFF ALONE.

ALTHOUGH THE HIPPO HAS A BULKY BODY AND SHORT LEGS, IT CAN GALLOP LIKE A HORSE IF NECESSARY.

THE PIGMY HIPPOPOTAMUS
THIS ANIMAL IS HALF THE SIZE OF THE HIPPOPOTAMUS YOU HAVE JUST MET. IT SPENDS LESS TIME IN THE WATER. THAT'S WHY ITS EYES AND NOSTRILS ARE NOT RAISED HIGH ON ITS HEAD.

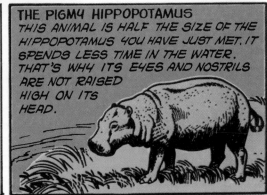

PRAYER TO GOD *

Remember little Ramu's prayer mentioned in my letter in TINKLE No. 14? Here are prayers from our readers. Each of them will receive Rs. 10/- from TINKLE.

—Editor

I pray that instead of seven periods of horrible studies and one period of fun and games, we should have seven periods of fun and games and one period of horrible studies.

Anirudh Goel
B-188, East of Kailash,
New Delhi 110065.

I pray to God to give me knowledge to help me in answering any type of question including 'Tinkle Tricks and Treats' and win prizes always.

B. Ravi Srinivas
3-6-325, Hyderguda,
Hyderabad 500001.

I pray every morning that Arithmetic should vanish from this world.

Pravanjan Mohanty
B/36 Sec-18 RKL-18
Sundargarh, Orissa 769 003

God sends snowfall to distant hills and valleys of Kashmir and Himachal. I am going to pray to Him to send snowfall to Chandigarh itself so that I and all the children here can play in the snow.

Miss Madonna Devasahayam
House No. 515/16D,
Chandigarh.

I want to eat sweets, cakes and pastries every day, and not get a stomach-ache. I want to eat icecream everyday, and not get a cold. I'd rather eat fruits than lunch or dinner, and always be the winner!

Farookh Bharucha
A-21, Royal Apartments, 7th floor, Khanpur,
Ahmedabad 380001.

* Refer to the footnote under the Editor's Note

Batsman's Prayer

O God!
Make me the best batsman.
Let cricket fans forget Botham and Bradman.
Spectators at stadium,
Forget your boredom
At slow-moving game.
Marvel at my score
In just half an hour
Of a sparkling century
Clap! clap! for my sixers
Only bless me, O God with specs
Fitted with s-l-o-w m-o-t-i-o-n glasses!
Lo! Even the world's fastest bowler's
Ball for me will be slow!

Sanjeev Dhavale
2/8 Ganesh Niketan, Prof. V.S. Agashe Path,
Dadar Portuguese Church, Dadar,
Bombay 400 028.

(Dear Sanjeev, in case God answers your prayer, please send the s-l-o-w m-o-t-i-o-n glasses to our cricketers now touring England.— Editor)

EDITOR'S CHOICE

S. Shyam Prasad

My young friends,

S. Shyam Prasad of Gulbarga recently sent us a story about two close friends, an elephant and a tailor. Every day the tailor would give a banana to his friend and the elephant would bring back a red lotus for him, from a pond near by.

One April Fools' day, the tailor as usual offers his friend a banana. And as usual the elephant begins to eat it. But suddenly he writhes in pain. The tailor had hidden a needle in the banana ! As the tailor roars with laughter, the elephant quietly walks away. Sometime later he comes back, as usual, with a lotus. As the tailor reaches for the lotus, the elephant showers dirty, muddy water on him.

All of us love to laugh and make others laugh. Sometimes to have a good laugh, one might, like the tailor, even hurt others. Such jokes are bad. They are cruel. A joke should make people laugh and not cry.

Affectionately yours,

Uncle Pai

PETROLEUM

Script: Luis M. Fernandes
Illustrations: Anand Mande

WE NEED KEROSENE TO COOK OUR FOOD WITH.

WE NEED PETROL AND DIESEL FOR OUR CARS AND TRUCKS.

WE NEED LUBRICANT OILS FOR MACHINES. ALL THESE AND MORE — COME FROM PETROLEUM.

PETROLEUM IS ALSO CALLED CRUDE OIL OR JUST, OIL.

SCIENTISTS SAY THAT PETROLEUM WAS FORMED FROM DEAD BODIES OF TINY ANIMALS AND PLANTS THAT LIVED MILLIONS OF YEARS AGO.

IT IS USUALLY FOUND DEEP DOWN IN THE GROUND.

BUT OCCASIONALLY IT IS FOUND ON THE SURFACE TOO. PETROLEUM FOUND ON THE SURFACE SOMETIMES CHANGES INTO A STICKY BLACK SUBSTANCE CALLED BITUMEN. BABYLONIANS COATED THEIR BOATS WITH BITUMEN TO MAKE THEM WATERPROOF.

ANCIENT INDIANS USED IT TOO, BUT AS A MEDICINE. THEY CALLED IT 'EARTH-BUTTER'.

FROM 1850 ONWARDS MANY FACTORIES CAME UP IN ENGLAND AND AMERICA. THE MACHINES IN THESE FACTORIES NEEDED OIL.

THE PETROLEUM FOUND ON THE SURFACE WAS NOT ENOUGH. AND SOON PEOPLE BEGAN TO DIG DOWN INTO THE EARTH FOR IT. THE FIRST OIL WELL WAS DRILLED IN 1859 IN AMERICA.

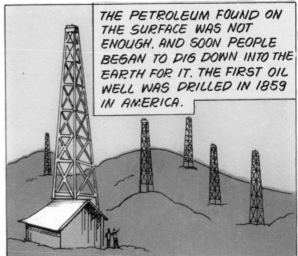

TODAY THE LEADING OIL-PRODUCING COUNTRIES ARE THE U.S.A., VENEZUELA, THE U.S.S.R., SAUDI ARABIA, KUWAIT, IRAN AND IRAQ.

IN INDIA, OIL IS FOUND MAINLY IN ASSAM, GUJARAT...

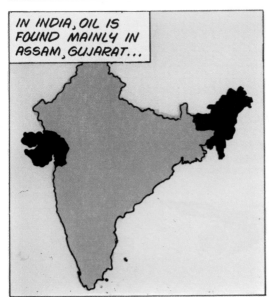

...AND OFF THE WEST COAST OF INDIA.

WHEN OIL IS TO BE DUG FOR, A TOWER OF STEEL GIRDERS IS FIRST BUILT OVER THE SPOT. THE TOWER IS CALLED AN OIL DERRICK.

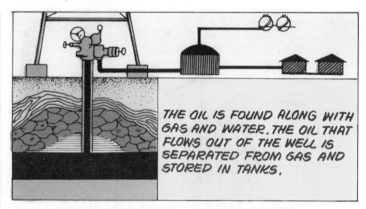

THE OIL IS FOUND ALONG WITH GAS AND WATER. THE OIL THAT FLOWS OUT OF THE WELL IS SEPARATED FROM GAS AND STORED IN TANKS.

THIS OIL IS THEN TAKEN TO A REFINERY WHERE IT IS SEPARATED INTO DIFFERENT SUBSTANCES LIKE PARAFFIN, DIESEL, KEROSENE, GASOLINE AND SO ON.

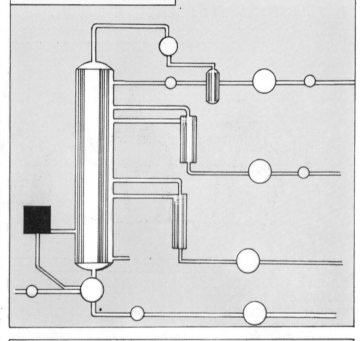

THE DERRICK IS USED FOR RAISING AND LOWERING THE DRILL.

BESIDES BEING A FUEL, OIL IS ALSO AN IMPORTANT RAW MATERIAL FOR THE CHEMICAL INDUSTRY. IT CAN BE TREATED WITH OTHER CHEMICALS AND CHANGED INTO PLASTICS, INSECTICIDES, DETERGENTS, EXPLOSIVES, COSMETICS, DYES AND EVEN DRUGS.

MAN-MADE RUBBER

DRUGS

COSMETICS

INSECTICIDES

POLISH

WAX

Kalia
THE CROW

Script:
LUIS

Illustrations :
PRADEEP SATHE

MEOWWW···

SOUNDS LIKE A KITTEN.

WHAT'S A KITTEN?

A KITTEN IS A YOUNG CAT.

OH!

BUT WHAT'S A CAT?

A CAT IS A BIG KITTEN.

YOU ARE SO CLEVER, CHAMATAKA. YOU KNOW EVERYTHING.

THERE IT IS!

LOOKS LIKE A BABY TIGER.

HELLO, ARE YOU LOST?

DON'T BE AFRAID. WE WON'T EAT YOU.

I'M GOING TO MY COUSIN'S HOUSE.

62

LET THAT LITTLE FELLOW GO, CHAMATAKA.

WHY SHOULD I? I'M HUNGRY.

CATCH HIS COUSIN. HE'S BIGGER. I KNOW WHERE HE LIVES.

TAKE US THERE THEN.

WE'LL CATCH HIS COUSIN TOO.

GOOD IDEA.

THIS IS THE CAVE.

C-CHAMATAKA!

S—SORRY! WE HAVE COME TO THE WRONG PLACE... HEH—HEH!

D—DON'T BOTHER TO GET UP. WE REALLY CAN'T STAY.

THAT'S NOT MY COUSIN. MY COUSIN IS A CAT.

WELL, THE TIGER IS A CAT TOO. BUT DON'T WORRY. I'LL HELP YOU FIND YOUR REAL COUSIN ONCE THOSE TWO ARE GONE.

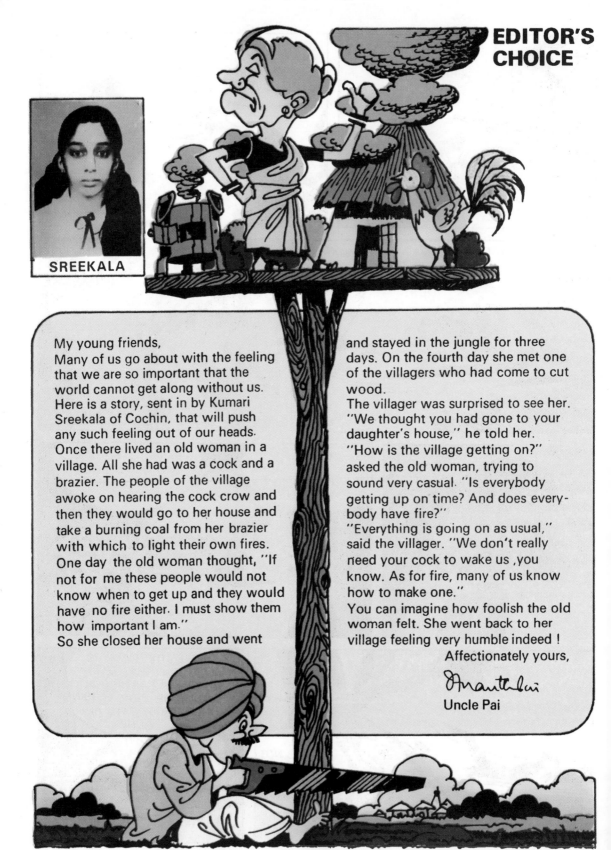

SREEKALA

My young friends,
Many of us go about with the feeling that we are so important that the world cannot get along without us. Here is a story, sent in by Kumari Sreekala of Cochin, that will push any such feeling out of our heads.

Once there lived an old woman in a village. All she had was a cock and a brazier. The people of the village awoke on hearing the cock crow and then they would go to her house and take a burning coal from her brazier with which to light their own fires. One day the old woman thought, "If not for me these people would not know when to get up and they would have no fire either. I must show them how important I am."

So she closed her house and went and stayed in the jungle for three days. On the fourth day she met one of the villagers who had come to cut wood.

The villager was surprised to see her. "We thought you had gone to your daughter's house," he told her.

"How is the village getting on?" asked the old woman, trying to sound very casual. "Is everybody getting up on time? And does everybody have fire?"

"Everything is going on as usual," said the villager. "We don't really need your cock to wake us ,you know. As for fire, many of us know how to make one."

You can imagine how foolish the old woman felt. She went back to her village feeling very humble indeed !

Affectionately yours,

Uncle Pai

64

NO. 18

Rs. 2.50

TINKLE

AMAR CHITRA KATHA

THE CHILDREN'S MONTHLY FROM THE HOUSE OF AMAR CHITRA KATHA

PUNYAKOTI

THE GENEROUS HOST

INTRODUCING ORIGAMI

MEET THE KOEL

READERS' MAIL

About 50 letters in one week. Close to 200 letters in one month. Nearly 25000 letters in one year. That's the number of letters *Tinkle* received in its first year of publishing. There's a common phrase that's always mentioned in the offices of *Tinkle*: the reader is key. As adults attempting to write children's content, the divide between the content and the reader can be quite vast. However, that has never been a problem at *Tinkle*.

As *Tinkle* embarked on its maiden voyage, the feedback from its readers started flowing in. Kids wanted to know how they could help hurry the publication of the next issue. They wanted the number of their delivery person so they could chide them for taking too long. But most of all they just wanted to talk. If you glance at some of their feedback you'll see the innocence in the children that wrote in.

Tinkle readers weren't left empty-handed for their efforts. Each reader received some kind of *Tinkle* merchandise for every letter they sent in. "Liked the recent Kalia the Crow story? Have a Kalia mask! Had a problem with one story? Thank you for your feedback. Please accept this *Tinkle* t-shirt as a measure of our gratitude." If that wasn't enough, readers also received a hand-written reply from Uncle Pai.

Readers' Mail that appeared in the magazine was filtered. It featured everything from criticism, praise and queries to stories about the readers and their lives. There was always another reason to look forward to the Readers' Mail page. Due to layout issues, each reader feedback would come with its own single gag. These gags were largely drawn by Pradeep Sathe, Ram Waeerkar and V. B. Halbe. They remain some of the best insights into these legendary artists' minds.

Readers' Mail

I love reading 'Tinkle'. But when I start reading, it finishes very soon. So please, Uncle, increase at least six pages more. In Tinkle No. 17 you did not introduce us to any animal.

Sheetal Joshi
Mathura Cantt

Readers' Mail

Your Tinkle is becoming very popular month by month and I think that it would never stop. But why don't you make a separate book of Kalia the Crow?

Mandar S. Vaidya
Vishakhapatnam-8

Readers' Mail

I am an 18-year-old boy. My friends, seeing me read Tinkle laugh at me. But I think this magazine is for all ages and NOT only for children

Rajiv Ajitsaria
Shillong

Readers' Mail

The Japanese papercraft Origami was the best. I am happy that you started it. I did the boat and asked my neighbour friend to do it and if he could I bet on my Tinkle magazine. To my surprise he did it. I had to give my beloved Tinkle, but he said. "No, Amar! I don't want it. I have bought one." "But," I said, "I was the first to buy the TINKLE in the bookstall. It had just come when I got there." "But I was the second," he replied.

Amar Heblekar
Ponda, Goa

THE OLIVE JAR

Based on a story from The Arabian Nights

Script: Shruti Desai
Illustrations: Dilip Kadam

LONG LONG AGO THERE LIVED TWO MERCHANTS, ALI AND HASAN.

ONE MORNING ALI CALLED ON HASAN WITH A JAR.

I AM GOING TO MECCA. WILL YOU KEEP THIS JAR OF OLIVES FOR ME?

CERTAINLY.

YOU CAN KEEP IT IN MY WAREHOUSE. HERE'S THE KEY.

ALI WENT TO HASAN'S WAREHOUSE...

...AND KEPT HIS JAR IN A CORNER.

SOON AFTERWARDS, ALI SET OUT FOR MECCA.

AFTER THE PILGRIMAGE HE DID NOT RETURN HOME IMMEDIATELY BUT WENT ON TO EGYPT AND OTHER COUNTRIES.

WHEN ALI DID NOT RETURN FOR SEVEN YEARS, HIS FRIEND, HASAN THOUGHT THAT HE WAS DEAD.

WHAT SHOULD I DO WITH HIS JAR OF OLIVES?

THEY MUST BE SPOILT AFTER ALL THESE YEARS. I'LL TAKE A LOOK.

JUST AS I THOUGHT. THEY'RE MOULDY.

WHAT A WASTE! IF I KNEW HE WASN'T COMING BACK... HUH!

GOLD COINS!

OH! THAT ROGUE!

A FEW MONTHS LATER, HASAN WAS STANDING OUTSIDE HIS SHOP WHEN—

HASAN! HASAN!

66

···TOOK IT HOME. THERE—

MY COINS ARE GONE!

HOW COULD HASAN DO THIS TO ME— HIS FRIEND!

ALI WENT TO HASAN'S HOUSE.

PLEASE RETURN MY GOLD TO ME.

WHICH GOLD?

THERE WERE A THOUSAND GOLD COINS IN MY JAR.

IN YOUR JAR?

BUT YOU TOLD ME IT CONTAINED ONLY OLIVES.

OH, COME, HASAN! DON'T PRETEND.

RETURN MY GOLD AND I WON'T BREATHE A WORD OF THIS TO ANYONE.

I DIDN'T TAKE YOUR GOLD.

NOW PLEASE GO AWAY. I HAVE WORK TO DO.

ALI WENT TO THE CALIPH, HAROON-AL-RASHID.

THIS IS A DIFFICULT CASE.

I NEED TIME TO THINK. THE MATTER OVER. COME AGAIN TOMORROW. BRING THE JAR OF OLIVES WITH YOU.

THE NEXT DAY WHEN ALI WENT TO THE CALIPH'S COURT—

I HAVE SUMMONED YOUR FRIEND TOO... AH, HERE HE IS!

YESTERDAY WHILE I WAS WALKING THROUGH THE STREETS OF BAGHDAD...

...I WATCHED THIS BOY PLAYING WITH HIS FRIENDS.

I FOUND HIM TO BE EXTREMELY CLEVER. I HAVE DECIDED THAT HE WILL TRY YOUR CASE.

LET US BEGIN.

ALI TOLD THE BOY HIS STORY. WHEN HE HAD FINISHED—

YOU WERE AWAY FOR SEVEN YEARS?

YES.

AND THE JAR WAS IN YOUR FRIEND'S WAREHOUSE ALL THAT TIME?

YES.

WHERE IS THE JAR?

HERE.

LET SOME MERCHANTS DEALING IN OLIVES BE BROUGHT IN.

SOME MERCHANTS WERE BROUGHT TO THE PALACE.

PLEASE EXAMINE THESE OLIVES.

HOW OLD ARE THOSE OLIVES?

ABOUT SEVEN MONTHS.

CERTAINLY NOT MORE THAN NINE MONTHS.

I AGREE.

YET ALI WAS AWAY FOR SEVEN YEARS!

SOMEBODY MUST HAVE REPLACED THE OLIVES.

PARDON ME, GREAT CALIPH. MY GREED GOT THE BETTER OF ME.

THE CLEVER BOY WAS REWARDED...

...HASAN WAS IMPRISONED...

...AND ALI GOT BACK HIS THOUSAND GOLD COINS.

71

THE GOAT'S MEDICINE

Story: Dr. S. Patel
Illustrations: V. B. Halbe

IN A FOREST THERE LIVED A GOAT. ONE DAY SHE WAS GOING TO HER NIECE'S HOUSE WITH A POT OF HONEY WHEN SUDDENLY—

TCHA! IT HAS STARTED TO RAIN!

I'LL WAIT IN THAT CAVE TILL IT STOPS.

PHEW! I'M DRENCHED!

OH!

WELCOME! DON'T BE AFRAID.

WE TOO HAVE COME IN BECAUSE OF THE RAIN.

THEY CAN'T FOOL ME. SOON THEY'LL POUNCE ON ME AND EAT ME UP.

I MUST MAKE THEM LEAVE... SOMEHOW...

73

YIEEIE!

WAIT!

HE DOESN'T WANT YOU TO BECOME STRONGER.

THE SELFISH CREATURE!

I'LL BRING HIM BACK AND WE'LL PULL OFF HIS TAIL.

YOU SHOULD BE GRATEFUL TO ME.

WHY?

I SAVED YOU FROM THE LION.

IT'S A TIGER'S HEART AND NOT A JACKAL'S TAIL WHICH HAS TO BE PUT INTO THIS MEDICINE.

CENTURY!
Illustrations: Ram Waeerkar

Based on a story sent by Yashesh Asher, Bombay

SHETH SHANKARLAL HAD NEVER PLAYED CRICKET. BUT ONE DAY HE FELT LIKE TRYING HIS HAND AT THE GAME.

GUNDYA!

YES, SAHEB.

LET'S PLAY CRICKET.

CRICKET?!

YOU BOWL AND I'LL BAT.

THEY BEGAN THE GAME...

...AND SHETH SHANKARLAL MANAGED TO HIT ONE OF THE BALLS.

ONE!

GUNDYA!

TWO...

...THREE

YES, MEMSAHEB?

GO TO THE MARKET AND GET ME A KILO OF ONIONS.

THE SERVANT FORGOT ABOUT THE GAME AND WENT TO THE MARKET.

WHEN HE CAME BACK—

...99...

...100!

I HAVE DONE IT! I HAVE HIT A CENTURY!

77

TINKLE TRICKS & TREATS

TTT-20

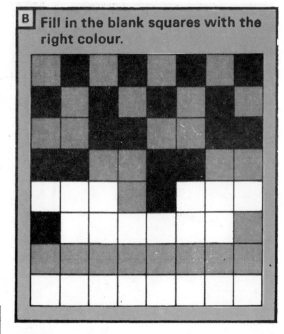

B
Fill in the blank squares with the right colour.

A
Find the odd man out.

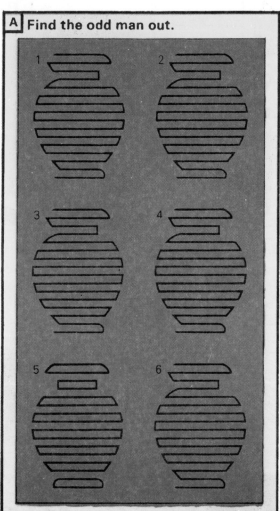

C
What is the major mistake in this picture?

SOLUTIONS TO TTT-20

A-5. B.

C.-
The
Taj Mahal
should be
white

78

Have you ever held a frog race ? Get your friends together and ask each one to bring a piece of thin card—6 cms x 9 cms. Fold the card as shown.

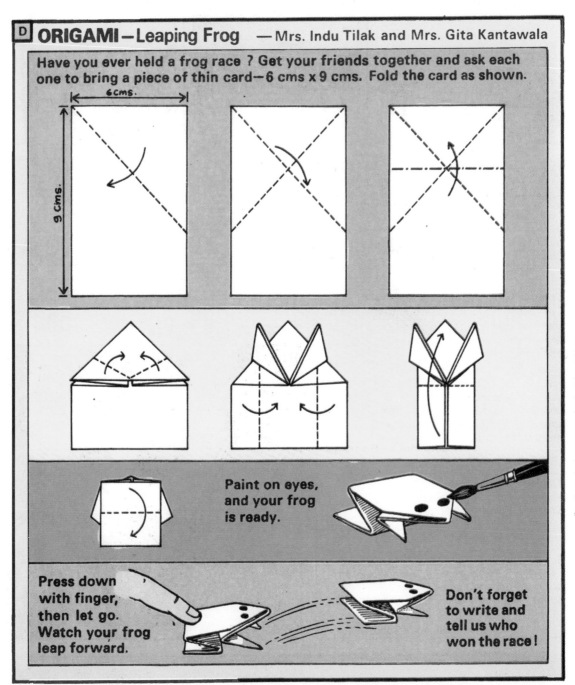

Paint on eyes, and your frog is ready.

Press down with finger, then let go. Watch your frog leap forward.

Don't forget to write and tell us who won the race !

*Refer to the footnote under the Editor's Note

RULES[*]

1. Mail your entries (entry form given overleaf) to:
   Tinkle (Competition Section), Post Box No. 1382, Bombay 400001.
2. With your entry you could send a self-addressed stamped (50 paise) envelope and collect an animal sticker. You will also receive a gift coupon if yours is an all—correct entry.
3. When you collect **3** such labels you could exchange them for a colourful animal mask.

Mooshik
From an idea suggested by Ramesh T. Vinchhi, Bombay.

Readers' Mail

I am an 18-year-old boy. My friends, seeing me read Tinkle laugh at me. But I think this magazine is for all ages and NOT only for children

Rajiv Ajitsaria
Shillong

Though I am completely satisfied with TINKLE, I have one suggestion to make and that is to give an incomplete story (of animals or so) and leave it to us to complete it.

Anupama M. Bahulkar
Ahmedabad

Why is Kalia always good, and Chamataka and Doob—Doob always bad? Will you send Chamataka and Doob—Doob to me? I will make them good.

Shardul P. Ramaiya
Bombay

Tinkle ! Tinkle ! Tinkle
You are such a lovely sight
That my brother and I fight.

Amitabh Mathur
New Delhi

In TINKLE (No. 16) "Mooshik" and "Monkey's Fast" were very interesting. In our class debating competition, by telling about "Monkey's Fast", I secured IInd prize.

G. Ganesh
Secunderabad

"For every problem, there is a solution." Yes, it is true. Before I subscribed for Tinkle, I could send the entries only on the 14th or 15th of every month. But nowadays I receive Tinkle quite early.

M. C. Deepak
Shillong

Please give your complete address in your letters if you want a reply. 　　-Editor

See and smile

CUT HERE- - - - - - - - - - - - - -

ENTRY FORM*

NAME _____

ADDRESS _____

_____

_____ PIN ☐☐☐☐☐☐

**MY SOLUTIONS
TO TTT-20:**

A _____

C _____

_____

B

MEET THE **FROG**

Based on the material provided by Nandini Deshmukh
Script : Ashvin • Illustrations : Pradeep Sathe

IT'S THE RAINY SEASON. THROUGH THE GENTLE PITTER-PATTER OF THE RAINDROPS YOU OFTEN HEAR A STRANGE SOUND.

IT'S THE CROAK OF A MALE FROG, SEEKING A MATE. HIS VOCAL SACS ARE LARGE SO HIS CROAK CAN BE HEARD ALMOST A KILOMETRE AWAY.

THERE'S SOMETHING MOVING THROUGH THE GRASS. IS IT A FEMALE FROG?

NO! IT'S A SNAKE! AND SNAKES EAT FROGS!

USING HIS LONG, STRONG, HIND LEGS HE TAKES ONE GREAT LEAP...

...AND LANDS ABOUT THREE FEET AWAY ON HIS SHORT FORELEGS.

ONE MORE LEAP AND HE IS SAFE IN THE WATER.

HIS HIND LEGS HELP HIM MOVE FAST IN THE WATER TOO!

HIS WEBBED FEET ACT AS EXCELLENT PADDLES.

AFTER A WHILE HE VENTURES OUT OF THE WATER AND CONTINUES TO CROAK.

THIS TIME, ANSWERING HIS CROAK, A FEMALE FROG COMES HOPPING TOWARDS HIM. BUT, BECAUSE THEY HAVE NO VOCAL SACS, FEMALE FROGS CANNOT CROAK AS DEEPLY OR LOUDLY AS MALE FROGS.

BOTH OF THEM JUMP INTO THE WATER. THERE THE FEMALE FROG LAYS HER EGGS.

SHE LAYS HUNDREDS OF THEM. EACH EGG HAS A THICK JELLY-LIKE COATING. THIS COATING HELPS THE EGGS TO STICK TOGETHER IN THE WATER.

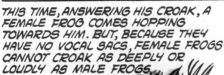

FROM NOW ON THE EGGS ARE ON THEIR OWN. FATHER AND MOTHER FROG LEAVE THEM IN THE WATER AND WANDER AWAY.

FATHER FROG HAS SEEN FLIES! THE FAVOURITE FOOD OF FROGS!

HE OPENS HIS MOUTH AND FLIPS OUT HIS LONG STICKY TONGUE. THE INSECT GETS STUCK TO IT.

OUR FROG'S MOUTH SNAPS SHUT AND THE INSECT IS SWALLOWED. FROGS EAT OTHER INSECTS AND WORMS TOO.

LET'S LEAVE THEM TO THEIR MEAL AND SEE WHAT'S HAPPENED TO THE EGGS. THEY HAVE BEGUN TO GROW BIGGER, AND TO TAKE THE SHAPE OF BEANS.

IN ABOUT A WEEK THEY HATCH. A TINY CREATURE CALLED A 'TADPOLE' WRIGGLES OUT OF EACH JELLY COVERING. IT'S LESS THAN HALF AN INCH LONG! IT CAN CLING ONTO A WATER PLANT.

VERY SOON TINY FRINGES CALLED GILLS APPEAR AT THE SIDES OF ITS HEAD. TADPOLES NEED THESE GILLS FOR BREATHING IN WATER.

SOON THE TADPOLE DEVELOPS EYES AND A MOUTH TOO.

IN TIME TWO LEGS GROW OUT FROM NEAR ITS TAIL.

LATER TWO FRONT LEGS APPEAR AND ITS LUNGS BEGIN TO DEVELOP.

WHEN ITS LUNGS ARE FULLY DEVELOPED, IT COMES OUT OF THE WATER. BUT IT STILL HAS A STUB OF A TAIL.

FINALLY ITS TAIL DISAPPEARS AND THE YOUNG FROG IS READY TO FACE ITS LIFE — A LIFE FULL OF ENEMIES LIKE BIG FISHES, BIRDS, SNAKES AND MAN. MAN USES FROGS FOR SCIENTIFIC EXPERIMENTS AND DISSECTIONS AND HE CONSIDERS FROG LEG MEAT A DELICACY.

IN THE HOT, DRY SEASON FROGS LIVE IN DEEP WATER OR BURY THEM- SELVES IN MUD AT THE BOTTOM OF A POND. THIS IS CALLED SUMMER SLEEP.

THOUGH A FROG HAS LUNGS IT ALSO BREATHES THROUGH ITS SMOOTH, MOIST SKIN. THE FROG IS AN AMPHIBIAN. AN AMPHIBIAN IS AN ANIMAL THAT CAN LIVE ON LAND AS WELL AS IN WATER.

82

THE REWARD

Illustrations: G. R. Naik

Based on a story sent by S. Badrinath

ONE DAY A FARMER WENT TO HIS FIELD.

ARE MY EYES PLAYING TRICKS ON ME?

I'VE NEVER SEEN A PUMPKIN AS LARGE AS THIS.

I'LL GIVE IT TO OUR KING.

THE KING WAS PLEASED WITH THE GIFT.

THIS MUST BE THE BIGGEST PUMPKIN IN THE WORLD!

GIVE HIM A THOUSAND GOLD PIECES.

THE FARMER IS A LUCKY MAN INDEED!

NEWS OF THE FARMER'S GOOD FORTUNE REACHED THE EARS OF A RICH MISER.

A THOUSAND COINS FOR A MERE PUMPKIN?

I WONDER WHAT HE WOULD GIVE ME IF I OFFERED HIM THIS COSTLY NECKLACE.

CARTLOADS OF GOLD...

...OR DIAMONDS!

THE MISER WENT TO THE PALACE...

...AND GAVE THE NECKLACE TO THE KING.

IT'S BEAUTIFUL!

WHAT CAN I GIVE YOU IN RETURN? GOLD? DIAMONDS?

NO, YOU ARE A RICH MAN AND WOULD NOT CARE FOR SUCH THINGS.

AH, I KNOW WHAT I CAN GIVE YOU!

THE PUMPKIN!

THE MISER, CLUTCHING THE HEAVY PUMPKIN STUMBLED OUT OF THE PALACE IN A DAZE.

FIRE FIGHTING

Script:
Luis M. Fernandes
Illustrations:
Chetna Shah and
Milind

THREE THINGS ARE NECESSARY TO MAKE A FIRE — OXYGEN, FUEL AND HEAT.

TO PUT OUT A FIRE IT IS ENOUGH TO TAKE ANY ONE OF THESE THINGS AWAY FROM THE OTHER TWO.

A SHORT-CIRCUIT HAS CAUSED A FIRE IN THIS MAN'S HOUSE.

HE IS TRYING TO PUT IT OUT BY THROWING WATER ON IT.

THIS IS THE WRONG THING TO DO BECAUSE ELECTRICITY CAN TRAVEL THROUGH WATER AND HE COULD GET ELECTROCUTED.

FORTUNATELY FOR HIM SOMEBODY HAS CALLED THE FIRE STATION AND THE FIREMEN COME RUSHING IN.

THEY PUT OUT THE FIRE WITH FIRE-EXTINGUISHERS.

FIRE-EXTINGUISHERS ARE OF VARIOUS TYPES. THIS FIREMAN IS USING ONE WHICH SPRAYS A DRY CHEMICAL POWDER ON THE FLAMES. THE CHEMICAL POWDER CUTS OFF THE OXYGEN SUPPLY TO THE FIRE.

EVERY CITY AND TOWN HAS ITS FIRE-BRIGADE. IN INDIA, THE FIRST FIRE STATION WAS SET UP IN BOMBAY, AROUND 1855. IT WAS RUN BY THE POLICE.

WHEN THE FIRE-ALARM RANG, TRAINED HORSES RAN FORWARD AND STOOD BEFORE THE CARRIAGE WHICH CARRIED THE STEAM-ENGINE.

THE STEAM-ENGINE WAS NEEDED TO FORCE A STREAM OF WATER UPWARDS THROUGH THE HOSE.

THE HORSES WERE HARNESSED AND THE FIRE-ENGINE TOOK OFF.

PEOPLE WATCHING IT GO CALLED IT 'BAMBA' WHICH IS A LOCAL WORD FOR STEAM-ENGINE. EVEN TODAY, A FIRE STATION IS CALLED 'BAMBAKHANA' IN MARATHI AND HINDI.

THE DAYS OF THE HORSE-DRAWN STEAM-ENGINE ARE LONG SINCE OVER. NOW THE FIRE STATIONS OF OUR MAJOR CITIES HAVE THE MOST MODERN FIRE-ENGINES.

87

WHEN THERE IS A FIRE, FIREMEN FIRST TRY TO SAVE PEOPLE'S LIVES. SOMETIMES PEOPLE ARE MADE UNCONSCIOUS BY THE SMOKE AND THEY HAVE TO BE CARRIED OUT.

IT IS ONLY AFTER THE PEOPLE ARE RESCUED THAT FIREMEN TRY TO SAVE PROPERTY.

BESIDES PUTTING OUT FIRES, FIRE-MEN ARE ALSO CALLED TO HELP WHEN A BUILDING COLLAPSES ... ... OR WHEN PEOPLE ARE TRAPPED IN LIFTS AND OTHER PLACES.

THEY ALSO HELP RESCUE BIRDS AND ANIMALS WHO ARE IN DIFFICULTY.

SOME DOS AND DON'TS
IF A PERSON'S CLOTHES ARE ON FIRE, HE SHOULD DROP TO THE GROUND AND START ROLLING. IF HE RUNS AROUND IN PANIC, TRIP OR PUSH HIM TO THE GROUND AND THEN SMOTHER THE FIRE WITH A THICK CLOTH, CARPET, CUSHION OR BLANKET.

IN CASE FIRE IS CAUSED BY AN ELECTRICAL GADGET DO NOT THROW WATER ON IT. JUST SWITCH OFF THE MAINS.

DO NOT PLAY PRANKS WITH THE FIRE-BRIGADE.

88

Kalia
THE CROW

Script:
LUIS

Illustrations :
PRADEEP SATHE

I WISH I COULD RUN AS FAST AS THAT DEER.

WHY DO YOU WANT TO RUN? I HAVE TOLD YOU SO OFTEN CHAMATAKA...

...LEARN TO FLY! LEARN TO FLY!

FLY AWAY YOURSELF, YOU IDIOT!

HE DOESN'T KNOW WHAT'S GOOD FOR HIM... I'LL TEACH HIM TO FLY SOMEHOW.

AHHA! THERE'S KALIA. PERHAPS I COULD LEARN THE SECRET OF FLYING FROM HIM.

ER... KALIA.

YES?

IS IT...ER... DIFFICULT TO FLY?

NO. WHY?

A FRIEND OF MINE IS...

HELP!

OH-OH, KEECHU AND MEECHU ARE IN TROUBLE.

WHAT'S THE MATTER?

EH? ER... DOOB-DOOB, WHAT WERE YOU SAYING ABOUT YOUR FRIEND?

AH, YES. MY FRIEND, CHAMATAKA IS SO SLOW THAT HE CAN'T CATCH...I...I MEAN, HE CAN'T ER...

IN SHORT, HE WANTS TO LEARN FLYING.

YES. NOT THAT HE WANTS TO CATCH ANIMALS...

I UNDERSTAND.

WELL IF YOU WANT TO TEACH HIM FLYING YOU HAVE TO HANG HIM UPSIDE DOWN FIRST.

UPSIDE DOWN?

LIKE THAT BAT.

OH! SO THAT'S THE SECRET.

MEANWHILE A FEW YARDS AWAY—

WE ARE TRAPPED. WHAT SHALL WE DO KEECHU?

L—LET'S RUN PAST HIM, WHEN HE GETS CLOSER.

YOU CAN'T ESCAPE!

NOW!

NOT SO FAST!

YOUR FRIEND GOT AWAY, BUT YOU WON'T!

AT LAST I'VE CAUGHT A RABBIT.

WHAM

HE'S OUT COLD.

BROTHER ELEPHANT COULD YOU HANG HIM UP FOR ME?

IT WOULD BE A PLEASURE!

OH, THE THINGS I DO FOR CHAMATAKA...

...BUT WHAT ARE FRIENDS FOR AFTER ALL.

THE CLEVER JUDGE

Based on a story sent by Renuka Dennis
Illustrations : M.N. Nangre

PEDRO LIVED WITH HIS GRANDMOTHER. THEY WERE VERY POOR. EVERYDAY HIS GRANDMOTHER MADE SOME VADAS...

...AND THE BOY TOOK THEM TO THE MARKET TO SELL.

ONE AFTERNOON HE WAS RETURNING HOME AFTER SELLING THE VADAS...

...WHEN HE SAW AN OLD WOMAN TRYING TO LIFT A BUNDLE OF WOOD ONTO HER HEAD.

WAIT, GRANDMOTHER. LET ME HELP YOU.

MAY GOD BLESS YOU, SON.

I AM GLAD I COULD HELP HER. SHE IS SO OLD.

92

HEY!

MY MONEY! IT'S GONE!

SOON SEVERAL VILLAGERS HAD GATHERED ROUND THE BOY.

WHERE DID YOU KEEP THE MONEY?

IN THIS BASKET.

ARE YOU SURE IT'S GONE? LET ME SEE.

UGH! YOUR BASKET IS SO OILY.

I SELL VADAS.

WHAT'S GOING ON HERE?

IT'S SENHOR CAETANO.

SENHOR CAETANO WAS A JUDGE. WHEN HE LEARNT ABOUT THE THEFT—

DID YOU SEE ANYONE NEAR THE BASKET?

NO, SIR.

YOU SAW NO ONE, YET THE MONEY IS MISSING.

THAT STONE MUST HAVE TAKEN IT.

?!

BRING IT TO THE COURT.

HAS THE JUDGE GONE MAD? HOW CAN ANYONE PUT A STONE ON TRIAL?

LET'S SEE HOW HE DOES IT.

EVERYONE WANTED TO ENTER THE COURT TO WATCH THE PROCEEDINGS BUT THE JUDGE STOPPED THEM AT THE GATE.

WAIT!

REQUEST THAT WOMAN TO LEND US THAT BUCKET OF WATER AND BRING IT TO ME.

WHEN THE BUCKET OF WATER WAS BROUGHT TO HIM —

PLACE IT HERE.

ANYONE WHO WANTS TO COME INTO THE COURT MUST DROP A COIN INTO THE BUCKET.

SEVERAL PEOPLE DROPPED A COIN EACH···

···AND ENTERED THE COURT.

THEN A STRANGER CAME FORWARD···

···AND DROPPED A COIN INTO THE BUCKET.

HE IS THE THIEF!

WHA···

95

THE MAN TRIED TO RUN AWAY BUT THE VILLAGERS CAUGHT HIM.

PLEASE LET ME GO!

GIVE THE BOY HIS MONEY.

H...HERE!

HOW DID YOU KNOW HE WAS THE THIEF, YOUR HONOUR?

MONEY KEPT IN THAT BASKET IS BOUND TO GET OILY.

WHEN HE DROPPED THE COIN INTO THE WATER A RING OF OIL SPREAD OUT FROM IT.

SO I KNEW HE WAS THE THIEF.

PEDRO RAN HOME BURSTING TO TELL HIS GRANDMOTHER ABOUT HIS ADVENTURE.

VASANT HALBE

Mr. Vasant Halbe, better known as V.B. Halbe, worked as an artist for *Amar Chitra Katha*. His illustrations were semi-realistic in style. They were closer to caricatures and cartoons than real versions of people or animals.

Initially the *Tinkle* Editorial Team was skeptical about him, when then Art Director Pradeep Sathe suggested him as the artist for Shikari Shambu*. However, Mr. Sathe insisted on him and with just his first sketches, Mr. Halbe won the Editorial Team over. He went on to illustrate Shikari Shambu stories for 15 years.

His art made the pages of *Tinkle* richer. His slightly exaggerated form of expressions added to the appeal of a story. He also gave form to the loveable smart alec, Anwar and the miserly Jagannath and his daughters Ina, Mina, Mynah, and Mo.

Mr. Halbe was a man of few words but he was well known for his humorous one-liners. This humor came through in his art, which remains rib-tickling to this day.

*A conservationist and a wildlife expert

A TALE OF TWO GIFTS
—A folktale from China

Script: Luis M. Fernandes
Illustrations: Ram Waeerkar

ONE DAY IN CHINA MANY CENTURIES AGO, AN OLD WOMAN'S DAUGHTERS-IN-LAW CAME TO HER.

WHAT IS IT, MY BLOSSOMS?

WE WISH TO GO TO···TO···

···TO THE CITY···TO VISIT OUR PARENTS.

OH!

THEY WENT TO THE CITY ONLY LAST MONTH.

I MUST STOP THEM FROM GOING SO OFTEN. MY SONS BECOME SO UNHAPPY WHEN THEY ARE GONE.

YOU MAY GO. BUT YOU MUST BRING ME TWO GIFTS FROM THE CITY, YOU LOTUS BLOSSOM···

···MUST BRING ME FIRE WRAPPED IN PAPER.

AND YOU, PEARL BLOSSOM, MUST BRING ME WIND IN A PAPER.

97

IF YOU DO NOT BRING THE GIFTS YOU MAY NOT ENTER THE HOUSE.

THE TWO GIRLS HAD AN ENJOYABLE HOLIDAY IN THE CITY.

AND THEY FORGOT ALL ABOUT THE GIFTS THE OLD LADY HAD ASKED THEM TO BRING.

IT WAS ONLY ON THEIR WAY HOME SEVERAL DAYS LATER THAT THEY REMEMBERED.

OH, THE GIFTS!

FIRE WRAPPED IN PAPER AND…AND…

AND WIND… ALSO IN PAPER!

OH, HOW COULD WE HAVE EVER AGREED TO BRING SUCH GIFTS!

OH, LOTUS BLOSSOM, WHAT ARE WE TO DO NOW?

98

THE TWO YOUNG WOMEN SAT DOWN BESIDE THE ROAD AND BEGAN TO CRY.

SOMETIME LATER A GIRL RIDING A BUFFALO, CAME THAT WAY.

SHE ASKED THE TWO WOMEN WHY THEY WERE CRYING. AND WHEN THEY TOLD HER—

YOU CANNOT SOLVE ANY PROBLEM BY CRYING.

YOU HAVE TO USE YOUR WITS. COME TO MY HOUSE.

THE GIRL TOOK THE WOMEN TO HER HOUSE.

AND THERE SHE GAVE LOTUS BLOSSOM A BEAUTIFUL PAPER LANTERN.

LIGHT THE CANDLE IN IT.

WHEN THE CANDLE WAS LIT—

NOW WHAT DO YOU HAVE?

FIRE WRAPPED IN PAPER!

AND THIS IS FOR YOU.

WIND IN PAPER! OOOOH!

THE TWO WOMEN THANKED THE GIRL AND RUSHED HOME.

HAVE YOU BROUGHT THE GIFTS?

YES.

I AM VERY PLEASED WITH YOU.

YOU MUST GET ME ANOTHER TWO GIFTS THE NEXT TIME YOU GO.

WE...WE WON'T BE GOING TO THE CITY AGAIN SO SOON.

THE OLD LADY'S PLAN HAD WORKED!

P.W.

100

WORDS FOR WORDS

Story: P. Varadarajan   Illustrations: V. B. Halbe

A CITY DWELLER WAS PASSING THROUGH A VILLAGE.

THE PEOPLE HERE ARE SO SIMPLE.

I COULD EASILY MAKE SOME MONEY HERE IF I TRIED.

LET ME BEGIN WITH THIS MAN. HE APPEARS TO BE RICH... AND FOOLISH.

OH, WHAT A NOBLE FACE YOU HAVE, SIR!

I CAN TELL THAT YOU ARE A MAN OF GREAT GENEROSITY.

WIFE, BRING TEN MEASURES OF RICE FOR MY FRIEND HERE!

MEN LIKE YOU ARE RARE, SIR. YOU SHINE LIKE A JEWEL ON A HEAP OF COAL.

WIFE, BRING A HUNDRED RUPEE NOTE.

LET ME RECITE A VERSE IN YOUR HONOUR, SIR.

FLOWERS BLOOM ONLY FOR A FEW HOURS; CLOUDS POUR ONLY FOR A FEW DAYS; RIVERS FLOW ONLY FOR A FEW MONTHS;

...BUT YOUR GLORY, SIR, SHINES FOREVER.

WIFE!

BRING TWO SILK DHOTIES.

102

HOW EASILY I HAVE FOOLED, THIS STUPID FELLOW!

ER...WHY HAVEN'T THE GIFTS COME AS YET, SIR.

GIFTS?

NOW, WHAT DID YOU DO WITH YOUR WORDS?

I ...ER... MADE YOU HAPPY.

WELL, I HAVE MADE YOU HAPPY WITH MINE.

WHAT MORE DO YOU WANT?

Halbe

THE MAN REALISED THAT THE VILLAGERS WERE NOT AS SIMPLE AS THEY LOOKED AND HASTILY LEFT THE VILLAGE.

EDITOR'S CHOICE

Master Atul Garg

My young friends,

A barber was going to a distant village. At noon he sat under a tree and unwrapped the rotis he was carrying. He had just bitten into one when a monkey came by.

"I have some butter," said the monkey.

The barber continued to chew his rotis.

"Here take it," said the monkey. "Spread it on your rotis."

So the barber took the butter from the monkey and spread it over his rotis and ate them.

Sometime later the barber got up to go.

"Take me with you," said the monkey.

"I can't," said the barber.

"Then return my butter!" said the monkey.

So the barber had to take the monkey along. On the way they saw a man selling bananas.

"Buy me a banana," said the monkey to the barber.

"I can't buy you a banana," said the barber.

"I have very little money."

"Then why did you eat my butter?" demanded the monkey. "Buy me a banana or return my butter."

So the barber bought the monkey a banana and they walked on. Sometime later they saw a man selling sweets.

"Buy me some sweets," ordered the monkey. The barber pretended not to have heard.

"Buy me some sweets or return my butter," screamed the monkey. The poor barber had to spend some more of his money on his companion. A little later they saw a wedding procession coming that way. The monkey fell in love with the bride.

"Get me that bride!" commanded the monkey.

"That I can't do," said the barber.

"Get me that bride or return my . . . !"

W H A M !

The barber had finally lost his patience and he hit the monkey so hard that it fell flat on its back. It was terrified. It leaped to its feet and ran away, much to the relief of the barber.

People who force a small kindness upon you only to demand ten-fold in return should be dealt with firmly. That is what this story sent in by Atul Garg from Gwalior teaches us.

Affectionately yours,

Uncle Pai

104

TINKLE TRICKS & TREATS TTT-21

A

These children are celebrating Independence day. What is the major mistake in the picture?

B

One of these leaders gave us the words JAI HIND. Which leader was it?

1 Netaji Subhas Chandra Bose

2 Swami Vivekananda

3 Raja Rammohan Roy

C

Can you name these great freedom-fighters?

1

2

3

SOLUTIONS TO TTT-21

A—National flag is flown halfmast only on days of national mourning, not on Independence day

B-1

C-1 Bhagat Singh
2 Sardar Vallabbhai Patel
3 Lal Bahadur Shastri

105

Origami–Helmet
— Mrs. Indu Tilak and Mrs. Gita Kantawala

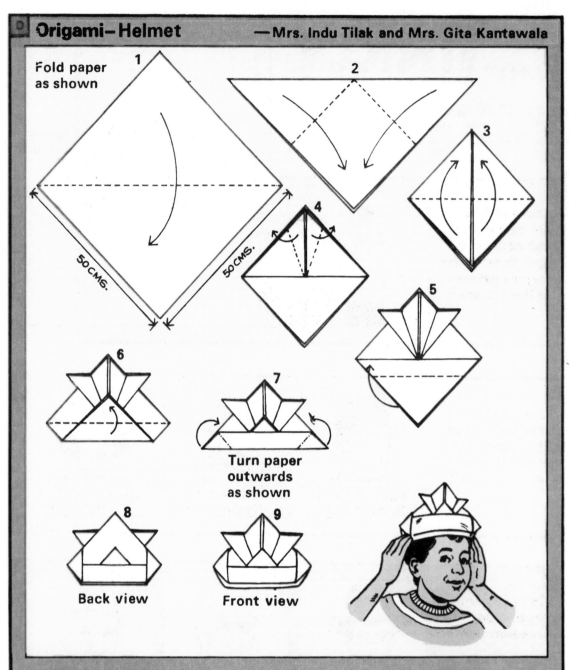

1 Fold paper as shown

50 CMS. 50 CMS.

2

3

4

5

6

7 Turn paper outwards as shown

8 Back view

9 Front view

* Refer to the footnote under the Editor's Note

Readers' Mail

I love reading 'Tinkle'. But when I start reading, it finishes very soon. So please, Uncle, increase at least six pages more. In Tinkle No. 17 you did not introduce us to any animal.

Sheetal Joshi
Mathura Cantt

I was very much disappointed when I bought Tinkle No. 17 and did not find the column 'Meet the Animal'. And Uncle, in this column why don't you print about rare animals? Then we will be able to know the habits and characters of the rare animals.

Yogesh Gupta
Bangalore

I am happy to read Tinkle. I enjoy it very much, but there are no adventures. I wish you would print some adventure serials. In order to read the complete story I will keep buying Tinkle.

B.S. Singh
Hospet

I like Tinkle very much. I am very unhappy because today when I read Tinkle No. 17 there was nothing like Meet the Butterfly or Meet the Tiger.

Jaideep Kataria
Poona

Uncle, I like Tinkle No. 17, especially the story of glass. But the story is very short. Next time when you publish stories about inventions, they should be long and interesting stories.

Nandini Kagoel
Bangalore

Please give your complete address in your letters if you want a reply.
—Editor

See and smile

*Refer to the footnote under the Editor's Note

THE MAN WHO WANTED 'NOTHING'

- A Nasruddin Hodja tale

Script: Luis M. Fernandes
Illustration: Ram Waeerkar

A MAN WAS TRYING TO LIFT A SACK ONTO HIS BACK WHEN A STRANGER CAME BY.

DO YOU NEED ANY HELP?

NO!

WHAT WILL YOU GIVE ME IF I HELP YOU?

NOTHING!

NOW GIVE ME MY REWARD.

WHAT REWARD?

I SAID I WOULD GIVE YOU NOTHING.

SO GIVE IT TO ME, GIVE ME 'NOTHING'.

HOW CAN ANYONE GIVE 'NOTHING'?

THEN WHY DID YOU PROMISE IT TO ME?

SOON A LARGE CROWD COLLECTED AROUND THE TWO MEN.

HE IS RIGHT.

NO! HE ISN'T!

FRIENDS, THE ONLY ONE WHO COULD SETTLE THIS MATTER IS THE HODJA.

SO THE TWO MEN WENT TO NASRUDDIN HODJA AND PUT THEIR CASE BEFORE HIM.

HE PROMISED ME 'NOTHING'. I WANT IT.

AND YOU SHALL HAVE IT.

LIFT UP THE CORNER OF THAT RUG, WILL YOU?

NOW WHAT DO YOU SEE UNDER IT?

NOTHING.

WELL, TAKE THAT 'NOTHING' AND GO AWAY.

The Digestive System

Your body is made up of millions and millions of tiny living cells. And every one of them needs food. This food is carried to them by your blood. But to enter your blood the food you eat has to be changed into a liquid. This change that the food you eat undergoes is called digestion.
The parts of your body that do this work are together called the Digestive System.

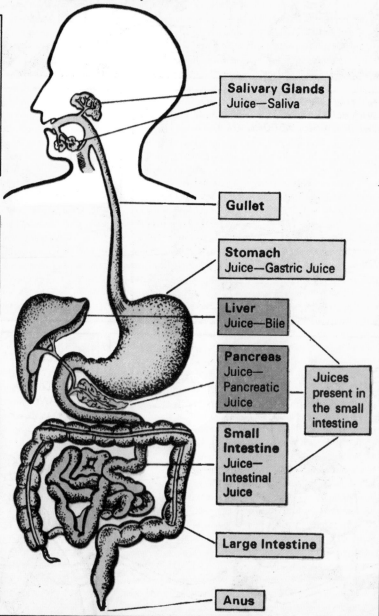

The many kinds of food you eat need different digestive juices to help them change into liquids. As soon as you put food into your mouth, your mouth begins to water. This water is the digestive juice called saliva and is produced by the salivary glands.

When you swallow your food it is pushed down your gullet into your stomach. There it is properly mixed with the digestive juices of your stomach and is then pushed into your small intestine.

The juices present in your small intestine complete the work of digestion. The digested food is absorbed through the walls of your small intestine into your bloodstream.

The waste is pushed into your large intestine and later out of your body through your anus.

Salivary Glands
Juice—Saliva

Gullet

Stomach
Juice—Gastric Juice

Liver
Juice—Bile

Pancreas
Juice—Pancreatic Juice

Juices present in the small intestine

Small Intestine
Juice—Intestinal Juice

Large Intestine

Anus

ROUNDWORMS

Based on
the material
provided by
Dr. S. G. Kabra

Illustrations:
G. R. Naik

RAMU IS EATING BHELPURI AT A ROADSIDE STALL.

NOT FAR AWAY, SOME ROUNDWORM EGGS ARE LYING IN THE DUST.

SUDDENLY, A GUST OF WIND BLOWS THEM ONTO RAMU'S BHELPURI.

RAMU CANNOT SEE THE EGGS BECAUSE THEY ARE VERY TINY. HE GULPS THEM DOWN ALONG WITH THE BHEL.

THE EGGS REACH RAMU'S STOMACH AND TRAVEL TO HIS SMALL INTESTINE...

LUNGS

HEART

STOMACH

LIVER

LARGE INTESTINE

SMALL INTESTINE

...WHERE THEY HATCH INTO LARVAE.

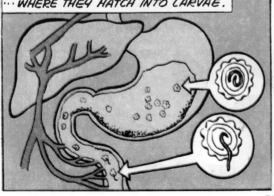

THE LARVAE THEN ENTER THE BLOOD VESSELS OF THE INTESTINE. THEY SWIM IN THE BLOOD TILL THEY REACH THE LIVER. AND HERE THEY REST FOR A FEW DAYS.

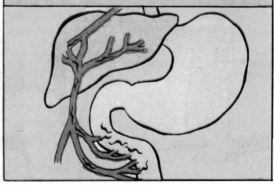

WHEN THEY ARE A LITTLE BIGGER THEY ENTER THE BLOODSTREAM AGAIN, GO UP TO THE HEART AND FROM THERE TO THE LUNGS.

IN THE LUNGS THEY ENTER THE AIR-SACS.

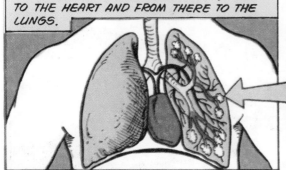

THE LUNGS, HOWEVER, DO NOT PROVIDE THEM WITH FOOD. THEY HAVE TO MOVE AGAIN. THEY BEGIN TO CRAWL UP THE AIR PASSAGE.

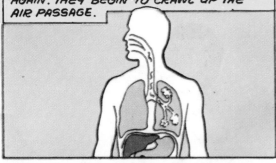

RAMU, MEANWHILE IS UNAWARE OF WHAT IS GOING ON IN HIS BODY. HE FEELS NO PAIN OR DISCOMFORT AND GOES ABOUT HIS WORK AS USUAL.

ONLY WHEN THE LARVAE REACH THE TOP OF THE AIR PASSAGE, DO THEY BOTHER RAMU. HIS THROAT TICKLES. HE COUGHS.

THE LARVAE ARE FORCED OUT INTO HIS MOUTH. HE SWALLOWS AND···

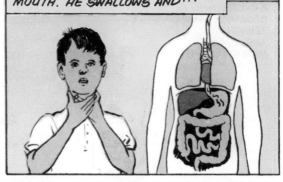

···THE LARVAE GO DOWN INTO HIS STOMACH··· AND FROM THERE TO THE SMALL INTESTINE. THEY ARE HOME AGAIN! SOON THEY MOULT AND BECOME ADULT WORMS. THERE'S PLENTY OF FOOD FOR THEM TO EAT, SO THEY GROW BIGGER AND BIGGER.

POOR RAMU DOES NOT KNOW THAT A PART OF THE FOOD HE EATS IS BEING EATEN UP BY THE WORMS. HE IS NOT GETTING PROPER NOURISHMENT AND HE LOOKS SICKLY.

HIS PARENTS SEE HIM TOSSING ABOUT RESTLESSLY AND GRINDING HIS TEETH IN HIS SLEEP. THEY BECOME WORRIED.

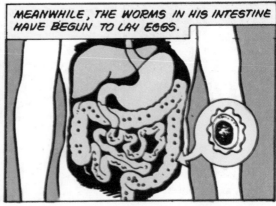

MEANWHILE, THE WORMS IN HIS INTESTINE HAVE BEGUN TO LAY EGGS.

WHEN RAMU GOES TO ANSWER THE CALL OF NATURE...

...SOME OF THESE EGGS PASS OUT WITH HIS STOOLS.

WHEN THE STOOLS DRY, THE EGGS ARE BLOWN AWAY BY THE WIND AND THEY LAND ON A CARTLOAD OF GUAVAS.

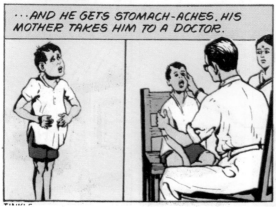

TO HER BAD LUCK, TINA BUYS JUST THE ONE ON WHICH A CLUSTER OF EGGS HAS SETTLED.

AND THE WHOLE CYCLE IS REPEATED IN HER BODY.

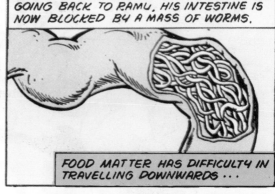

GOING BACK TO RAMU, HIS INTESTINE IS NOW BLOCKED BY A MASS OF WORMS.

FOOD MATTER HAS DIFFICULTY IN TRAVELLING DOWNWARDS...

...AND HE GETS STOMACH-ACHES. HIS MOTHER TAKES HIM TO A DOCTOR.

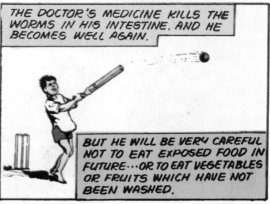

THE DOCTOR'S MEDICINE KILLS THE WORMS IN HIS INTESTINE. AND HE BECOMES WELL AGAIN.

BUT HE WILL BE VERY CAREFUL NOT TO EAT EXPOSED FOOD IN FUTURE...OR TO EAT VEGETABLES OR FRUITS WHICH HAVE NOT BEEN WASHED.

RANI RABBIT AND PAYAL PIG

Script:
Raj Kinger

Illustrations:
V. B. Halbe

RANI RABBIT WAS A VERY OLD RABBIT. SHE LIVED IN A TINY HOUSE WITH A YARD FULL OF PAPAYA TREES.

ONE DAY SHE HAD A VISITOR— PAYAL PIG.

RANI RABBIT, RANI RABBIT, PLEASE GIVE ME A PAPAYA.

I WILL IF YOU HELP ME WASH MY HOUSE.

I WILL! I WILL!

THEY SET TO WORK.

OH, I'M SO HUNGRY! CAN I HAVE A SLICE OF THAT PAPAYA?

OF COURSE!

SOON—

DELICIOUS! DELICIOUS!

AFTER A WHILE—

OOH! I FEEL SO TIRED. I'LL JUST HAVE A NAP.

PAYAL TOOK ONE LOOK AT THE SLEEPING RANI...

···GRABBED THE PAPAYA···

···AND RAN AWAY AS FAST AS HE COULD.

THE NEXT DAY PAYAL WAS BACK AT RANI'S YARD.

RANI RABBIT, WILL YOU GIVE ME A PIECE OF PAPAYA?

GO AWAY, YOU BAD PIG! YOU TOOK MY PAPAYA AND DIDN'T COMPLETE YOUR WORK.

OH, PLEASE! I PROMISE TO DO ALL THE WORK TODAY.

ALL RIGHT. HELP ME HANG UP THESE CLOTHES.

SOON—

OH, I FEEL SO HUNGRY. CAN I HAVE A SLICE OF PAPAYA?

RANI RABBIT WENT IN AND CAME OUT WITH A PAPAYA.

HERE YOU ARE!

WHILE YOU EAT THAT, I'LL FETCH ANOTHER BUCKET OF CLOTHES.

THAT WAS ALL PAYAL NEEDED.

THE NEXT DAY GREEDY PAYAL WAS BACK AT RANI'S DOOR.

RANI RABBIT, WILL YOU PLEASE GIVE ME SOME PAPAYA?

RANI RABBIT'S EYES GLEAMED.

OH, YES, PAYAL. WAIT A MINUTE. I HAVE A LARGE PAPAYA FOR YOU.

PAYAL LICKED HIS LIPS AND WAITED.

WHY CAN'T SHE HURRY?

JUST A MOMENT, PAYAL.

WHERE IS THE PAPAYA?

HERE!

YOU WICKED PIG!

TAKE THIS···

···AND THIS··· AND THIS···

···AND···

HELP! HELP!

Halbe

116

Kalia
THE CROW

Script:
LUIS

Illustrations:
PRADEEP SATHE

SEE WHAT I FOUND IN THE VILLAGE! IT'S CALLED A FOOTBALL.

WHAT IS IT GOOD FOR?

YOU HAVE TO HIT IT AROUND.

LIKE THIS.

LET ME TRY! LET ME TRY!

NOT SO HARD, YOU IDIOT! NOW LOOK WHAT YOU'VE DONE!

WE'LL NEVER FIND IT AGAIN!

YOU CROCODILES HAVE NO SENSE AT ALL.

HE'S JUST ENVIOUS BECAUSE I HIT IT SO FAR. HE'S LUCKY I AM SO UNDERSTANDING.

THE MAGIC SLIPPER

—A tale from Japan

Story retold by Hema Pande
Illustrations: Ram Waeerkar

POOR KENTARO WAS WORRIED. HIS MOTHER WAS ILL.

HE HAD NO MONEY TO BUY MEDICINE AND FOOD FOR HER.

I'LL HAVE TO GO TO UNCLE AGAIN FOR MONEY. I HOPE HE WILL HELP.

AT HIS UNCLE'S —

WHAT! YOU AGAIN?

PLEASE, UNCLE...

OUT!

POOR KENTARO SAT DOWN BY THE ROADSIDE AND BEGAN TO WEEP.

HE WEPT AND WEPT TILL HE FELL ASLEEP.

SUDDENLY—

WHAT ARE YOU DOING HERE, LITTLE ONE?

BEFORE KENTARO STOOD AN OLD MAN.

MY MOTHER IS ILL AND I HAVE NO MONEY TO···TO TAKE CARE OF HER.

IF I DON'T BUY HER SOME MEDICINE SOON··· SHE WILL SURELY DIE.

DON'T WEEP, I'LL HELP YOU.

TAKE THIS WOODEN SLIPPER. WHEN YOU PUT IT ON AND JUMP, A GOLD COIN WILL FALL OUT OF IT.

BUT REMEMBER, NEVER TAKE OUT MORE THAN ONE COIN AT A TIME BECAUSE···

···EACH TIME YOU JUMP, YOU WILL SHRINK A LITTLE. AFTER A REST, YOU WILL BE YOURSELF AGAIN.

BUT TAKE OUT TOO MANY COINS AT ONCE AND YOU'LL BECOME AS TINY AS A MOSQUITO.

THE NEXT MOMENT THE OLD MAN VANISHED AND KENTARO AWOKE WITH A START.

WAS...WAS I DREAMING? BUT NO—THE WOODEN SLIPPER IS HERE!

I'LL GO HOME AND TRY IT OUT.

AS SOON AS HE REACHED THE COURTYARD OF HIS HOME HE PUT ON THE SLIPPER...

...AND JUMPED.

OH...!

RAP

A GOLD COIN DID FALL OUT! HOW HAPPY I AM! I CAN NOW BUY RICE, MEDICINES, ANYTHING, FOR MOTHER. SHE WILL BE WELL AGAIN.

THE WHOLE VILLAGE CAME TO KNOW OF KENTARO'S MAGIC SLIPPER AND EVERYONE WAS HAPPY FOR HIM. BUT NOT HIS UNCLE!

I MUST GET THAT SLIPPER FOR MYSELF! NOW!

HE WENT TO KENTARO'S HOUSE.

GOOD DAY, GOOD DAY, MY NEPHEW!

WELCOME, UNCLE.

KENTARO AND HIS MOTHER GAVE HIM A DELICIOUS MEAL.

EXCELLENT FOOD! AH! UM··· AHEM··· I HEAR YOU HAVE A MAGIC SLIPPER THAT GIVES GOLD COINS.

I DO, UNCLE. I'LL SHOW IT TO YOU.

THIS IS THE SLIPPER, UNCLE!

WILL YOU SELL IT TO ME? I'LL PAY YOU ANYTHING YOU WANT.

HEH—HEH! LET'S ALSO FORGET ABOUT ALL THE MONEY YOU OWE ME. WHAT DO YOU SAY, EH?

THIS SLIPPER WAS GIVEN TO ME BY A KIND, OLD MAN. I CANNOT SELL IT TO YOU.

THEN AT LEAST LEND IT TO ME FOR A DAY.

NO! NO, UNCLE! I CANNOT.

OH, COME NOW...

JUST FOR A DAY, NEPHEW, I'LL RETURN IT TOMORROW.

UNCLE! WAIT!

THE UNCLE HURRIED HOME. HE SPREAD A MAT ON THE GRASS IN HIS INNER YARD.

WILL IT REALLY WORK?

I CAN'T BELIEVE IT!

RAP

HE JUMPED AGAIN.

124

BEAUTIFUL, SHINING, LOVELY, GOLD COINS!

BESIDE HIMSELF WITH JOY, THE UNCLE JUMPED AND JUMPED...

RAP RAP RAP RAP

...TILL SOON, A PILE OF GOLD COINS LAY ON THE MAT.

HO HO HO! I'LL BE THE RICHEST MAN IN JAPAN.

I'M TIRED. I'LL REST FOR A WHILE, THEN START ALL OVER AGAIN.

SUDDENLY—

WHAT'S THIS? THAT GOLD COIN... IT LOOKS AS BIG AS A MAT!

WHY, NOW! THIS PILE LOOKS LIKE A MOUNTAIN OF GOLD! IT'S HIGHER THAN FUJIYAMA!

FRIGHTENED, HE LOOKED ALL AROUND HIM.

THE TREES ARE TOUCHING THE SKY! GOOD HEAVENS! WHAT IS HAPPENING?

I CANNOT SEE THE END OF MY GARDEN! THE HOUSE LOOKS GIGANTIC!

JUST THEN, KENTARO ARRIVED THERE. HE LOOKED FOR HIS UNCLE ALL OVER THE HOUSE. THEN AT LAST, IN THE BACK YARD—

WHAT A PILE OF COINS!

BUT WHERE HAS UNCLE GONE?

UNCLE, UNCLE... WHERE ARE YOU?

THEN A THOUGHT STRUCK KENTARO.

COULD IT BE THAT UNCLE, BY TAKING OUT ALL THESE GOLD COINS, HAS NOW BECOME AS TINY AS A MOSQUITO? IS THAT WHY I CAN'T SEE HIM?

WHAT'S THIS ON THE SLIPPER? IT LOOKS LIKE A LITTLE BEETLE...

UNCLE—YOU! OH, NO! HOW TERRIBLE!

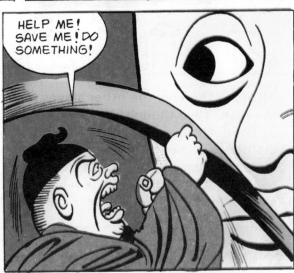

HELP ME! SAVE ME! DO SOMETHING!

BUT KENTARO COULD NOT EVEN HEAR HIS UNCLE'S SHOUTS.

POOR UNCLE! I CAN DO NOTHING TO HELP HIM. HIS GREED HAS BROUGHT HIM TO THIS SORRY STATE.

KENTARO PUT THE HEAP OF GOLD COINS INTO A BAG AND WENT HOME AND HE AND HIS MOTHER LIVED HAPPILY EVER AFTER.

My young Friends,

Thousands of years ago a number of slaves were waiting to accompany their master on a long journey.

Finally the master was ready to go and the slaves scrambled for the baggage.

Nobody wanted to carry the heavy things, so they pushed and fought for the lightest pieces of luggage.

But one slave, a hunchback, went straight up to a large sack and hoisted it onto his shoulders.

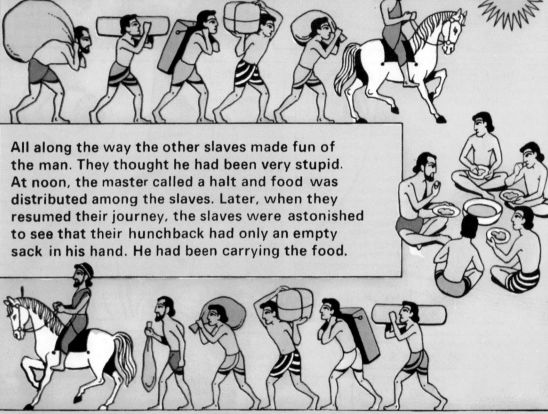

All along the way the other slaves made fun of the man. They thought he had been very stupid. At noon, the master called a halt and food was distributed among the slaves. Later, when they resumed their journey, the slaves were astonished to see that their hunchback had only an empty sack in his hand. He had been carrying the food.

This story has been sent in by reader Gopali R. Pathak of Baroda.

What Gopali perhaps does not know is that the slave she has written about was none other than Aesop.

Aesop later became a famous story-teller. One story of his which I am sure all of you know is that of the fox and the grapes!

Yours affectionately,

Uncle Pai

NO. 22

TINKLE

Rs. 2.50

THE
CHILDREN'S MONTHLY
FROM THE HOUSE OF
AMAR CHITRA KATHA

THE MAGIC SLIPPER

MEET THE TOUCAN

FOSSILS

ABOUT
READERS' CHOICE

Knowing what readers want is vital for a magazine's health. And for *Tinkle* the source of this information were the letters to the editor. Every day Uncle Pai was showered with letters from around the nation. In the hoard of these letters Team *Tinkle* often found what the readers desired.

These letters were filled with gratitude, suggestions and sometimes criticism. And none of these were taken lightly. If a reader asked for a feature on how radios worked or oil was found, it was promptly arranged for in a following issue. But this wasn't all. Readers were also given a chance to have their own stories published in the magazine.

These stories could be their original creations or stories that were narrated to them by their parents and grandparents. The readers were asked to pledge that they hadn't read these stories anywhere but only heard them narrated. This soon proved to be a fantastic way of finding little known folk tales. These folk tales were perhaps never written down, but merely passed down generations by word of mouth. They now found home in the pages of *Tinkle*, under the label of 'Readers' Choice'. These folk tales were permanently recorded on paper and in the minds of thousands of readers who had never read or heard of them before.

The stories that were chosen were scripted by *Tinkle*'s staff writers. To encourage readers to send in their stories, they were given a small cash prize. As luck would have it, some of the stories were priceless! The readers on their part showed such enthusiasm that staff writers were seldom out of stories to script.

ONE EVENING A FOX WAS GOING HOME...

...WHEN HE FELL INTO A PIT.

AHH!

NOW HOW DO I GET OUT OF HERE?

HE BEGAN TO HOWL.

AFTER SOME TIME A LION PEERED IN.

WHAT'S THE MATTER?

WHY ARE YOU HOWLING LIKE THAT?

THE WORLD IS ABOUT TO COME TO AN END.

HOW DO YOU KNOW?

I HAD A DREAM.

ONLY THOSE IN THIS PIT WILL BE SAVED.

OH!

IF YOU DO YOU'LL BE THROWN OUT. JUMP IN.

THE FOX BEGAN TO HOWL AGAIN. SOON—

WHY ARE YOU HOWLING?

THE WORLD IS ABOUT TO BREAK INTO TWO.

ONLY THOSE WHO ARE IN THIS PIT WILL BE SAVED.

PLEASE LET ME JUMP IN TOO, FRIENDS,

ON ONE CONDITION.

YOU MUST NOT SNEEZE. IF YOU DO, YOU'LL BE THROWN OUT.

I NEVER. SNEEZE.

OUCH!

IT'S GETTING CROWDED IN HERE.

AA··· AAAH··· CHOO!

HE SNEEZED!

THROW HIM OUT

THE FOX, DELIGHTED TO BE OUT OF THE PIT, HURRIED HOME.

AND IT WAS A LONG TIME BEFORE THE OTHER ANIMALS REALISED THEY HAD BEEN TRICKED AND MANAGED TO GET OUT.

132

TINKLE TRICKS & TREATS
TTT-22

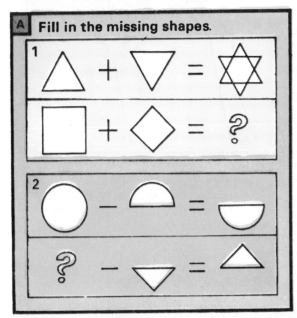

A — Fill in the missing shapes.

1

△ + ▽ = ✡

▢ + ◇ = ?

2

○ − ◠ = ◡

? − ▽ = △

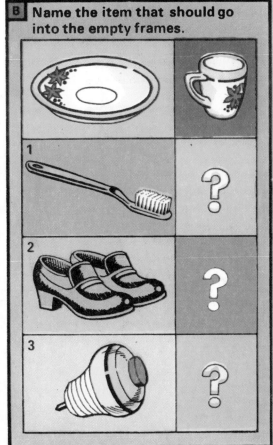

B — Name the item that should go into the empty frames.

1 ?

2 ?

3 ?

C — What is the major mistake in this picture?

1982
SEPTEMBER
31 FRI.

SOLUTIONS TO TTT-22

A – 1 ◇ inside square 2 ◇

B – 1 Toothpaste 2 Socks 3 String

C – September has only 30 days.

133

Make your own OASIS

D

You will need 4 or 5 pieces of paper 14 cms. x 24 cms. a long pencil, gum, a pair of scissors, a piece of cardboard for the base, sand and a piece of glass.

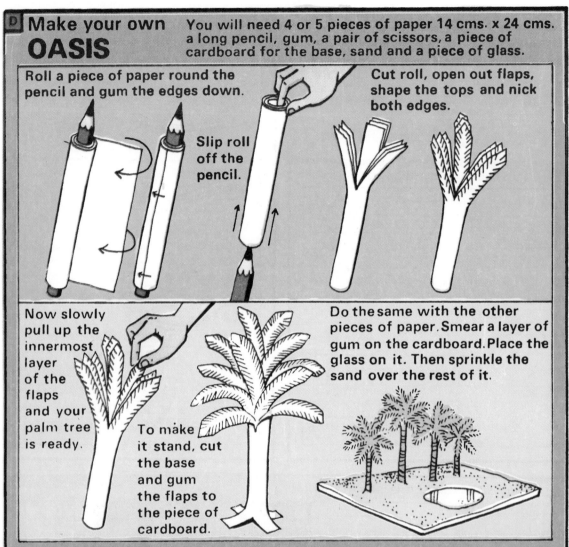

Roll a piece of paper round the pencil and gum the edges down.

Slip roll off the pencil.

Cut roll, open out flaps, shape the tops and nick both edges.

Now slowly pull up the innermost layer of the flaps and your palm tree is ready.

To make it stand, cut the base and gum the flaps to the piece of cardboard.

Do the same with the other pieces of paper. Smear a layer of gum on the cardboard. Place the glass on it. Then sprinkle the sand over the rest of it.

* Refer to the footnote under the Editor's Note

A PRIZE
FOR EVERY ALL CORRECT ENTRY! SEE RULES

The first hundred all-correct entries received by us will each win a copy of the Amar Chitra Katha title

ANDHER NAGARI
(dated 15th October 1982)

RULES*

1. Mail your entries (entry form given overleaf) to:
   Tinkle (Competition Section), Post Box No. 1382, Bombay 400001.
2. With your entry you could send a self-addressed stamped (50 paise) envelope and collect an animal sticker. You will also receive a gift coupon if yours is an all—correct entry.
3. When you collect **3** such coupons you could exchange them for a colourful animal mask.

Mooshik

STOP, READ, ACT

1. Tinkle Subscriptions: Hindi/Eng.

You can get TINKLE by post. The annual subscription rate for 12 issues is Rs. 25/- (add Rs. 3/- on outstation cheques). Drafts/cheques/M.O. should be in favour of India Book House Magazine Co.

Send your subscription giving your complete address and specifying the language to :

India Book House Magazine Co.,
249, Dr. D.N. Road, Bombay 400 001

Complaints regarding late receipt/non-receipt of TINKLE and also information regarding change of address should be sent to Uncle Martin of India Book House Magazine Co. at the address given above. Quote your subscription no. in your letter to Uncle Martin.

2. Readers' Mail

Letters to Uncle Pai can be sent either separately or along with Tinkle Tricks & Treats entries to the following address:

TINKLE (Competition Section)
Post Box No. 1382, Bombay 400 001

Please give your address if you want a reply.

3. Readers' Choice

Stories for the "Readers' Choice" feature should be sent separately (not with Tinkle Tricks & Treats entries) addressed to:

Editor
TINKLE-Readers' Choice
India Book House
29, Nathalal Parekh Marg
Rusi Mansion, Bombay 400 039

Send a self-addressed stamped envelope if you want the story to be returned. Please do not send photographs until asked for.
Rs. 25/- will be paid for every accepted story.

Please send only those folktales you have heard and not those you have read in books, magazines or textbooks. Along with the story please send the following letter:

Dear Uncle Pai,

I heard this story from—(my parent/uncle/aunt/etc). He/she too heard this story from someone else and did not read it in a book.

(Give your name & address in block letters)   My signature

*Refer to the footnote under the Editor's Note

- - CUT HERE -

TTT-22

ENTRY FORM*

NAME_____

ADDRESS_ _____

_____

_____

STATE_____

PIN ☐☐☐☐☐☐

MY SOLUTIONS:

A
1	2

C_____
_____
_____

B 1_____
2_____
3_____

_____
_____
_____

Readers' Mail

The Japanese papercraft Origami was the best. I am happy that you started it. I did the boat and asked my neighbour friend to do it and if he could I bet on my Tinkle magazine. To my surprise he did it. I had to give my beloved Tinkle, but he said. "No, Amar! I don't want it. I have bought one." "But," I said, "I was the first to buy the TINKLE in the bookstall. It had just come when I got there." "But I was the second," he replied.

Amar Heblekar
Ponda, Goa

I suggest that a feature could be started on the culture and traditions of India and other countries of the world.

Vidya
Hyderabad

The stories which have been published in Tinkle No. 18 are previously read. We had 'Punyakoti' as a lesson in VIth Std. in the Kannada text book. We also had 'The Generous Host' as a lesson in our VIIIth Std. in the non-detailed text book. So I humbly request you Uncle, not to publish stories which have already been written in books and read by many children.

Azra Fathima
Bangalore

I like Tinkle very much. In Tinkle No. 18 I liked the story 'Punyakoti' and the other 'The Generous Host'. I like Kalia the crow, Mooshik and See and Smile very much.

Rajesh D. Mittal
Bombay

I love your Tinkle book very much. For me there is no other comic except Tinkle. First my mother used to scold me but, oh what a change! Now she encourages me and my little brother to spend some time on reading your delightful book.
Vive la Tinkle!

Sarita Fernandes
Bombay

Sir, we request you to give some articles about space rockets and space shuttle. And also you can give some article about submarine and underwater animals and plants.

Shubhashish Daw &
Bhishma Chawla
Putta Parthi

Uncle, let us write to you frankly that the last issue made us very upset because nothing was interesting except TTT-17 and your letter. "Glass" was also very short. Uncle, for the vacation, you should give us more stories and new stories—let us say—A Holiday Special Issue.

Mrudank & Bhavesh
Jardosh
Surat

I think that the best magazine for children like me is Tinkle. I like to read TINKLE very much.
Why have you stopped 'Meet the Animals'? Please continue it. Also I want to read how TV and radio work. Please tell me.

G. Venkatesh
Jamshedpur

Please give your complete address in your letters if you want a reply.

Editor

See and smile

MEET THE **TOUCAN**
ILLUSTRATIONS : PRADEEP SATHE

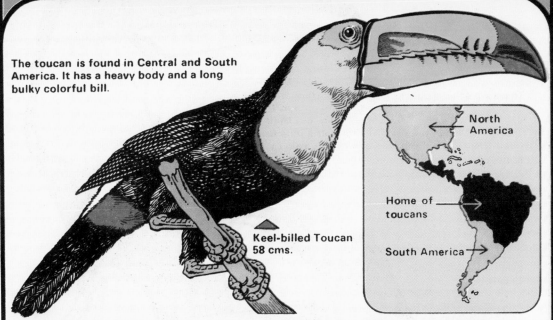

The toucan is found in Central and South America. It has a heavy body and a long bulky colorful bill.

Keel-billed Toucan 58 cms.

North America

Home of toucans

South America

You may think its bill is heavy. But it is not. It is made of a horny outer layer supported by a network of bony filaments. This makes its bill extremely light, but very strong.

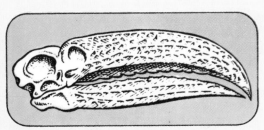

Nobody knows why its bill is so huge. But it comes in handy when the bird has to reach for fruit. Besides fruits, toucans eat insects, nestlings and occasionally, lizards.

The huge bill may also frighten away birds of prey and smaller birds whose nests the toucan wants to rob.

The toucan's large colourful bill attracts attention. So the bird takes care to hide it when it goes to sleep. It places the bill on its back and covers it with its drab tail. A sleeping toucan looks like a ball of feathers.

Toco Toucan
63 cms.

There are several species of toucans. Here are some of them. Though they vary in size and colour, their habits are the same. They cannot sing, but their loud croaks and harsh sounds carry for half a mile or more. They nest in hollow trees and lay two to four eggs.

Laminated Hill Toucan
43 cms.

Emerald Toucan
36 cms.

Double-collared Toucan
38 cms

How Hodja bought a donkey

— A Nasruddin Hodja tale

Script : Luis Fernandes
Illustrations : Ram Waeerkar

ONE DAY THE HODJA TOOK HIS DONKEY TO THE MARKET TO SELL...

...AND SOON FOUND A BUYER FOR IT.

I'LL GIVE YOU TWENTY-FIVE PIASTRES FOR IT.

ALL RIGHT.

THE MAN PAID HODJA THE MONEY...

...AND THEN IMMEDIATELY PUT THE DONKEY UP FOR SALE AGAIN.

COME FOLKS, LOOK AT THIS MAGNIFICENT BEAST.

SEE HOW STRONG AND HEALTHY IT LOOKS. AND IT IS SO GENTLE TOO.

I'LL GIVE YOU THIRTY PIASTRES FOR IT.

I'LL GIVE YOU THIRTY-FIVE.

FORTY!

EVERYBODY WANTS TO BUY MY DONKEY.

IT MUST BE A BETTER ANIMAL THAN I THOUGHT.

I'LL GIVE YOU FORTY-FIVE PIASTRES FOR IT..

I'LL GIVE FIFTY.

FIFTY-FIVE! SOLD! YOU CAN HAVE IT FOR FIFTY-FIVE PIASTRES.

SO HODJA BOUGHT BACK HIS OWN DONKEY...

...AND RODE AWAY, QUITE PLEASED WITH HIMSELF.

WHAT A HANDSOME DONKEY I HAVE!

KNOCK OUT!

Story: Rita Jaisingh
Illustrations: Ram Waeerkar

THE LION AND THE MOSQUITO

Illustrations: Vinay Sapre

Based on a story sent by Kamal Prasad, Guntakal (A.P.)

A MOSQUITO WAS BUZZING AROUND A LION'S HEAD.

AND THE LION GOT ANNOYED.

GO AWAY BEFORE I SQUASH YOU!

DON'T MAKE ME LAUGH.

I MAY BE SMALL BUT YOU ARE NO MATCH FOR ME.

LET'S FIGHT.

WHAT! YOU WANT TO FIGHT ME!

SPLAT!

WHOOSH!

HALF AN HOUR LATER —

HAD ENOUGH?

I... I... DON'T WANT TO HURT...

...A LITTLE CREATURE LIKE YOU.

I HAVE WON, HAVEN'T I?

BUT THE LION PRETENDED NOT TO HEAR AND QUIETLY SLUNK AWAY INTO THE BUSHES.

FOSSILS

Script: Luis M. Fernandes
Illustrations: Anand Mande

A MAN, DIGGING IN HIS FIELD, FOUND A PIECE OF AMBER...

...IN WHICH AN INSECT HAD BEEN TRAPPED.

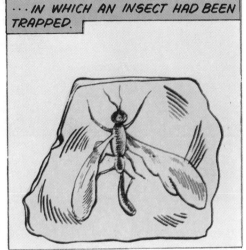

HOW DID THE INSECT GET INTO THE AMBER? THE STORY IS THOUSANDS OF YEARS OLD. THE INSECT WAS CRAWLING UP A TREE FROM WHICH A RESIN OR SAP WAS OOZING OUT...

...AND IT GOT TRAPPED IN THE RESIN.

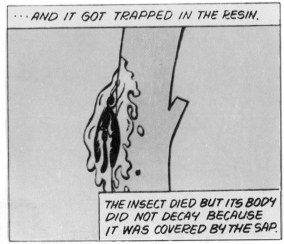

THE INSECT DIED BUT ITS BODY DID NOT DECAY BECAUSE IT WAS COVERED BY THE SAP.

THE NEXT DAY A STORM UPROOTED THE TREE. IT FELL TO THE GROUND...

... AND GOT COVERED WITH MUD.

IT LAY THERE CENTURY AFTER CENTURY. THE RESIN WHICH HAD OOZED OUT OF IT AND TRAPPED THE INSECT, CHANGED INTO THE MATERIAL CALLED AMBER.

JUST AS THE INSECT WAS PRESERVED IN AMBER, THIS MAMMOTH FOUND IN SIBERIA WAS PRESERVED IN ICE FOR CENTURIES.

THE PIECE OF AMBER, THE INSECT AND THE MAMMOTH ARE CALLED FOSSILS. ANYTHING LEFT OF A PLANT OR ANIMAL AFTER IT HAS BEEN DEAD FOR THOUSANDS OF YEARS, IS CALLED A FOSSIL.

THIS IS A FOSSIL OF A LEAF ...

...AND THIS OF A FISH.

IT IS BY STUDYING FOSSILS THAT WE KNOW ABOUT THE STRANGE ANIMALS WHICH LIVED THOUSANDS OF YEARS AGO.

EVEN AN OLD FOOTPRINT, PRESERVED IN THE GROUND FOR CENTURIES, CAN BE CALLED A FOSSIL. THIS IS A FOSSIL OF A DINOSAUR TRACK.

Kalia
THE CROW

Script:
LUIS

Illustrations:
PRADEEP SATHE

DOOB-DOOB, YOU AND I COULD MAKE A WONDERFUL TEAM. BUT YOU MUST LEARN TO HUNT.

I CAN HUNT VERY WELL, THANK YOU.

ONLY IN THE RIVER. YOU COULDN'T CATCH A FLY ON LAND. WHAT IF THE RIVER WERE TO DRY UP ONE DAY? YOU'D STARVE TO DEATH.

!!

IS IT...ER... DIFFICULT TO HUNT ON LAND?

IT'S NOT EASY. BUT I'LL TEACH YOU THE SECRETS.

WE JACKALS ARE BORN HUNTERS. I CAN SPOT MY PREY A MILE AWAY.

THEN HOW'S THAT I'VE NEVER SEEN YOU CATCH ANYTHING?

SSSSSH A FROG.

WATCH HOW I CATCH IT.

GOT YOU!

145

SEE HOW EASY IT WAS! YOU COULD CATCH BIGGER ANIMALS IN THE SAME WAY.

COME OUT, YOU!

???

ER···CHAMATAKA···I··· DON'T THINK···THAT'S A FROG.

Y—YOU'RE RIGHT!

S-SO SORRY, FRIEND. I THOUGHT YOU WERE SOME- ONE ELSE··· HEH-HEH!

ER···CHAMATAKA, I THINK I'VE LEARNT ENOUGH TODAY.

G-GOODBYE.

HELP!

THUMP THUMP THUMP

WHAT'S THAT?

ELEPHANTS STAMPEDING!

ELEPHANTS?

THUMP THUMP

I'D BETTER GET OUT OF THEIR WAY.

WHEW! THAT WAS A NARROW ESCAPE!

THUMP THUMP

YOU!

KALIA TOLD ME TO DO IT.

OH, I DIDN'T REALLY NEED HIS HELP.

I WOULD HAVE TIED THAT PYTHON INTO KNOTS IF IT HAD NOT LEFT ME.

CHAMATAKA, LOOK!

IT'S HIM AGAIN!

YIEEEEE...!

WHEN MOUNTAINS HAD WINGS

— A mythological tale

Script : Meera Ugra
Illustrations : Madhu Powle

LONG LONG AGO, MOUNTAINS HAD WINGS.

THEY COULD FLY ANY TIME, ANYWHERE.

ZOOM

THESE MOUNTAINS HAVE MADE OUR LIFE DANGEROUS!

YES. SOMETHING MUST BE DONE. LET US PRAY TO LORD INDRA.

AND SO, NOT LONG AFTER, THE DEVAS AND THE RISHIS PRAYED TO INDRA.

INDRA PROMISED TO HELP THEM.

HE SET OUT ON HIS FOUR-TUSKED ELEPHANT, AIRAVATA.

HE CHASED EACH MOUNTAIN...

...AND CUT OFF ITS WINGS WITH HIS WEAPON VAJRA, THE THUNDERBOLT.

AS EACH MOUNTAIN'S WINGS WERE CUT OFF, DOWN IT CAME WITH A THUD.

THUD

THUS, ONE BY ONE ALL THE MOUNTAINS FELL TO THE GROUND.

AND THERE THEY REMAIN TO THIS DAY.

150

MEET THE GORILLA

Script : Ashvin
Illustrations : Pradeep Sathe

THESE TRIBALS ARE WALKING THROUGH A JUNGLE IN AFRICA.

SUDDENLY THEY STOP AND RAISE THEIR SPEARS. A GORILLA! SHOULD THEY ATTACK OR SHOULD THEY FLEE?

OUR FRIEND MAKES THE FIRST MOVE. HE STANDS UP LIKE A MAN AND FACES THEM.

HE TEARS OUT BRANCHES AND LEAVES AND THROWS THEM INTO THE AIR.

HE THUMPS HIS MIGHTY CHEST.

THEN WITH A GREAT ROAR HE RUSHES FORWARD.

THE TREMBLING HUNTERS TURN AND FLEE.

OUR FRIEND HEAVES A SIGH OF RELIEF. ALL THAT GREAT SHOW OF FURY WAS ONLY A BLUFF TO CHASE THEM AWAY. HE FEELS QUITE PROUD OF HIMSELF.

FOR ALL HIS FIERCE LOOKS HE IS REALLY A GENTLE FELLOW AND WOULD LIKE TO AVOID A FIGHT IF POSSIBLE.

ONE OF HIS THREE WIVES WAS GIVING BIRTH TO A BABY. AS THE HEAD OF HIS TROOP OR FAMILY IT WAS HIS DUTY TO PROTECT HER. AND HE DID IT WELL.

HERE IS THE PROUD MOTHER HOLDING HER NEWBORN IN HER ARMS AND NURSING IT.

MEANWHILE THE OTHER MEMBERS OF THE FAMILY ARE BUSY HAVING A GOOD FEED TOO!

GORILLAS ARE STRICTLY VEGETARIAN. THEY EAT FRUITS, JUICY LEAVES, ROOTS AND BAMBOO SHOOTS.

THEIR HANDS ARE JUST LIKE OURS. FOUR FINGERS IN ONE DIRECTION AND THE THUMB IN ANOTHER.

THAT'S WHY THEY CAN HOLD AND PICK THINGS AS WE DO.

WHY, THIS FEMALE IS HOLDING A PLANT WITH HER FOOT!

THAT'S BECAUSE A GORILLA'S FEET ARE FORMED LIKE OUR HANDS AND NOT OUR FEET.

152

THIS ONE IS TEARING AWAY THE TOUGH COVERING OF A PLANT. HE CAN DO SO BECAUSE HIS CANINE TEETH ARE LONG AND SHARP.

BUT FOR THIS, A GORILLA'S TEETH ARE EXACTLY LIKE OURS IN SHAPE AND NUMBER.

FEEDING TIME IS OVER. OUR FRIEND IS READY TO MOVE ON. HE STANDS UP. THAT'S A SIGN TO HIS TROOP TO FOLLOW HIM.

YOU CAN SEE HOW WELL THE STRONGER MEMBERS OF THE TROOP PROTECT THE WEAKER MEMBERS AS THEY MOVE. THE FATHER LEADS. THEN COME THE YOUNGSTERS AND MOTHERS WITH BABIES. AND LAST OF ALL THE OTHER FEMALES.

EVEN A HUNGRY LEOPARD DOES NOT DARE ATTACK SUCH A UNITED FAMILY!

TOWARDS NOON THEY RELAX FOR SOME TIME. HERE'S MOTHER GORILLA CUDDLING HER NEWBORN BABY.

THESE TWO ARE BUSY CLEANING EACH OTHER'S FUR.

AT SUNSET TWO FEMALES START CLIMBING UP A TREE.

FATHER GORILLA IS PLAYING WITH THE YOUNG ONES.

THEY GET BUSY MAKING PLATFORMS OF INTERWOVEN BRANCHES WITH RIMS AROUND THEM. SOON IT WILL BE TIME TO GO TO BED.

THE YOUNGSTERS CLIMB UP THE TREE AND CHOOSE THEIR PLATFORMS. CHILDREN BELOW THREE ARE ALLOWED TO SHARE THEIR MOTHERS' PLATFORM.

THE LEADER WHO HAS TO GUARD HIS SLEEPING FAMILY HAS HIS PLATFORM ON THE LOWEST BRANCH.

GORILLAS SELDOM DRINK WATER BECAUSE THEY LIVE ON JUICY FRUITS AND PLANTS. BUT IF THEY COME ACROSS WATER THEY DIP AN ARM INTO IT AND SUCK THE WATER FROM THE FUR. THEY MAY EVEN USE EGG OR COCONUT SHELLS AS CUPS.

YOU MIGHT WONDER WHY GORILLAS WALK ON ALL FOURS WHEN THEY CAN STAND ERECT LIKE US. THEIR SPINES ARE STRAIGHT, NOT CURVED LIKE OURS AND THIS MAKES THEM TIRED IF THEY STAND FOR TOO LONG.

GORILLA

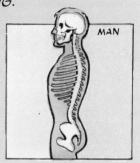

MAN

THE GORILLA, THE CHIMPANZEE, THE ORANG-UTAN AND THE GIBBON ARE ALL CALLED APES. APES HAVE NO TAILS, LIVE IN FAMILY GROUPS AND ARE MORE INTELLIGENT THAN MONKEYS.

THE CHIMPANZEE (AFRICA)

THE ORANG-UTAN (ASIA)

THE GIBBON (ASIA)

WHEN THE ELEPHANT WENT FISHING

Illustrations: V.B. Halbe

Based on a story sent by Pratima P. Mall, Bhawanipatna, Orissa

IN OLDEN DAYS ELEPHANTS HAD LONG, BUSHY TAILS.

ONE DAY AN ELEPHANT WAS WALKING PAST A FOX'S HOUSE WHEN HIS TAIL HIT THE ROOF OF THE HOUSE...

...AND KNOCKED IT DOWN.

YEOWW!

HAHAHAHA!

OH, MY GOD! MY BEAUTIFUL TAIL CUT!

SOME DAYS LATER THE ELEPHANT WAS PASSING BY A RIVER, WHEN...

... HE SAW THE FOX.

WHAT ARE YOU DOING?

I'M FISHING.

WHY DON'T YOU CATCH SOME FISH TOO?

I DON'T EAT FISH.

YOU'RE LUCKY BECAUSE YOU COULD NEVER CATCH ONE.

WHY NOT?

YOU HAVE TO BE VERY BRAVE TO CATCH FISH.

I AM BRAVE.

I'LL CATCH A FISH JUST TO SHOW YOU THAT I CAN.

WHAT DO I HAVE TO DO?

JUST PUT YOUR TAIL INTO THE WATER.

AND KEEP IT THERE AS LONG AS I KEEP MINE.

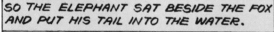

SO THE ELEPHANT SAT BESIDE THE FOX AND PUT HIS TAIL INTO THE WATER.

PRESENTLY—

OUCH! SOMETHING BIT ME.

IT MUST BE A FISH.

NOW COMES THE REAL TEST OF YOUR COURAGE. YOU MUST KEEP YOUR TAIL IN THE WATER NO MATTER WHAT HAPPENS.

THE FISH IN THE WATER BEGAN TO NIBBLE AT THE ELEPHANT'S TAIL.

OOOOH!

WHAT'S HAPPENED?

ARE YOU AFRAID?

NO! NO! ...HEH HEH.

THIS IS REALLY PAINFUL. BUT I MUSTN'T SCREAM. I MUST SHOW THIS FOX THAT I AM AS BRAVE AS HIM.

THAT'S ENOUGH.

THE FISH HAVE EATEN MY TAIL!

HELP!

THEY SAY THAT EVER SINCE ELEPHANTS HAVE HAD SHORT TAILS.

Halbe